CW00404103

Published by Long Midnight Publishing, 2020

ISBN: 9798640912876

The Elephant At The Table first appeared in The Sunday Express

The Case Of The Stained Glass Widow first published by Blasted Heath 2012

www.douglaslindsay.com

Cover Design by James, GoOnWrite.com

COLD SEPTEMBER

DOUGLAS LINDSAY

Contents

Aged Eight, Alice On The Shore

Prologue

The mosaic was being created in twelve separate panels. A maritime scene, the surface of the sea two thirds of the way up the picture. Above it, waves crashed, the clouds were dark, a fishing vessel pitched on white horses, angry men shouted. Beneath the waves, a sea of calm in glorious colour, at the heart of it a giant squid, long and slender, eight arms, two tentacles thrust forward.

Eleven of the panels had been completed. As there was only space on the workbench for a single panel, the others were stacked, in four bundles, against the workshop wall. Assembled, the mosaic would be twelve feet by six.

She had sketched the entire piece, then split it into manageable sections. She had completed each panel in turn; drawing the precise outline of the design, cutting the ceramic tiles and fixing them into place, then grouting the section when she was happy with the image.

Alice Hawkins had been working on the mosaic for twelve years. She was almost done.

The phone rang.

1

They ate in silence. The rhythm of the dinner table had changed as their children had grown. The rambunctiousness of toddlers to the questions of the under-tens, the arguments of early teens to the sullen, quickly-eaten dinners of youth, and now, now that they were gone, the heart of the dinner table had been ripped out, and there was nothing left to say.

They listened to film music during dinner. Every night. Michael's choice, of course. Alice liked the tunes well enough, but she would happily never listen to the theme to *Out of Africa* again.

When he wasn't there she sat in silence, listening to the sea, the occasional clang of the bell on the boat that was tied up and rarely used.

'How was your day?' he asked.

Water and wine, dinner was done, plates pushed aside. The music ended, and she could hear the waves on the rocks outside, the flutter of the breeze through the open window.

'A journalist called.'

That was her news. She hadn't waited with any anticipation to deliver it. He wouldn't be interested.

'Looking for me?'

'Asking about the mosaic.'

'Why?'

Silence, followed by the shimmering, urgent strings of *The Big Country*.

When she didn't immediately answer he followed with, 'Wasn't there a thing in the Journal already?'

He knew there'd been a thing in the local newspaper. He wasn't trying to hurt. He genuinely didn't understand why anyone cared.

'He's from the Times. He saw the Journal, thought it was worth a piece in one of the nationals. He's coming up on Thursday.'

'From London?'

Incredulity. She supposed it was something.

'Yes. I suggested he stay at the Highland.'

Michael had nowhere else to go with his surprise, so he

simply said, 'I'm going the other way.'

He smirked oddly, as though this was ironic.

'London?'

'Kent.'

'Writers' retreat?'

'Yes.'

They held the gaze for a moment, and then withdrew behind their wine glasses at the same time, self-consciousness about neither of them.

There was a conversation to be had, but it was too late; his heyday as a screenwriter, three hit television shows, followed by failure, and the waning of the muse, given way to speaking engagements and living off the past. He didn't need the money, but he did need the something-to-do of it.

They'd never talked about it. The rise and fall, like all great empires. The time when his phone hadn't stopped ringing, to now, this age, when the phone was something on which he read the news.

That evening he did the washing up, which only ever happened when he was feeling guilty. She wondered what he'd be doing in Kent, but didn't imagine it would involve intimacy with another woman. He'd seemed so disinterested in sex their entire married life, she could hardly imagine him pursuing anyone else.

2

Aged eight, Alice on the shore. The Fife coast, a small, sandy beach, framed by rocks.

Mist had rolled in from the sea, low and dense. The morning was still, bar the sound of the waves. Visibility no more than twenty or thirty yards. The only other sound came from a boat, tied to a jetty a short distance away, lost in the fog. Moving in the swell, the bell on the boat intermittently clanging. The sound of it anchored the scene in her memory.

The boy seemed to come from nowhere. In her later imagination he was conjured by the sea, but at the time he was just a boy playing on the beach.

She saw him standing by the water line, where the waves touched the shore, something at his feet, neither flotsam nor jetsam nor seaweed. She felt comfortable approaching, but when it came to it, she found herself simply staring at the thing washing in the waves.

After they had stood side by side for several minutes she said, 'Your shoes are soaking. Won't your mum be annoyed?'

'I'll leave them on the porch to dry.'

'Is it an octopus?' quickly followed, now that the conversational barrier had been broken.

'A squid. The body's a different shape. Longer and thinner.'

'Is it still alive?'

'I don't know.'

The body was two feet long, the arms trailed further ahead.

'It's young,' said the boy. 'The adults are bigger. Giant. It's a giant squid.'

He threw his arms out wide to indicate the prodigious size. She still remembered the thrill of it.

'Maybe we should push it back into the water,' she said, in thrall to the moment.

'It has nasty suckers on its arms,' said the boy. 'Even at this size, they'd hurt if they wrapped themselves around your hand.'

She took a small step backwards, hoped he wouldn't notice.

'But I think it might be dead, so you don't have to be afraid.'

'I'm not afraid.'

She retraced her short step so that she was standing beside

him, the squid's inert arms next to her red shoes.

Eventually they plucked up the courage to move the squid back out into open water. Alice kicked off her shoes. They held it gingerly, taking one side of the mantel each, and slowly moved it away from the sand, back into the waves.

When they were in shallow water, the squid now floating free, they let go and took a step away. The squid lay for a moment, and then suddenly, with a pulsing movement of its body, it moved smoothly away.

Alice squealed and splashed backwards. The boy stood still. Together they watched the squid on its way, until it had disappeared into grey water.

Time had been lost, and after a while she realised she was late for lunch, and that her mother, the worrier, would be nervous by the kitchen fireplace.

'Will you be here later?' she asked.

'Maybe.'

She left the beach, red shoes in her hand. She knew she wouldn't see him again, but later that afternoon she waited for him nevertheless.

* * *

Alice dreamed all her life of searching for the giant squid. Any giant squid that she could imagine was the one she'd helped from shore. But it was never about the giant squid.

3

'Wow, that is amazing!'

Not many people had seen Alice's work. Michael had, of course, in his stoic, genuine disinterest. Her mother, concerned that Alice had wasted so much time on such pointless frippery. A few family friends, unsure what to make of it. One work colleague of Michael's had seemed enthralled, until Michael had intervened to let him know better. Alice was to the Roman mosaicists of Cirencester what the self-published author was to Margaret Atwood.

The journalist had arrived twenty minutes earlier. They'd chatted in the kitchen while the old whistling kettle boiled. His name was Beckett. A few years younger than her. Slim, eyes the colour of a hazy summer blue sky, something of the Paul Newman about him. She felt the connection as they stood in the kitchen, smiled their way through the introductions, conventional talk of travel and writing and living by the sea.

Now he stood over the mosaic, which Alice had laid out on the floor of the workshop, the workbench pushed back, the last panel – a few small tiles and grouting short of being completed – inserted into place. Coffee mug in his left hand, he knelt down beside the mosaic and ran his fingers softly over the small pieces of tile.

Michael had never touched the mosaic. For some reason it reminded her of the way he had never touched her stomach when she'd been pregnant.

'The age-old conflict between light and dark,' he said. 'Yet you subvert the convention and the darkness of the ocean, by having the sea so full of colour and life. Above the waves, though…'

He let the sentence go, aware he was narrating the picture to its creator. Instead he indicated the top third of the mosaic; the grey sky, the dark world inhabited, and brought to ruin, by the human race.

'I like that you show the sea at its best. The beauty of it. The life, the colour, the diversity. No plastic bottles, no fishing lines, no chemical waste. And it's so intricate. The work that's gone into this, the skill…'

His fingers traced over the coral at the bottom of the sea, across the cluster of anemones, the riot of colourful fish, the ray, the eels, until he came to the giant squid. His fingers paused, his eyes ran the length of the beast, from the long, extended arms, down along the mantle to the two, small fins of the tail.

She watched his hands. She imagined his touch.

'Aristotle wrote of the giant squid,' he said.

'The teuthus.'

'You know your legends,' he said, smiling.

She couldn't remember anyone looking at her like that before, and for a moment it rendered her speechless.

'Tell me about the mosaic,' he said, quickly filling the gap, completely in tune with the rhythm of the conversation. Then, 'This is an amazing place to work. I mean, what a view! Oh my God.'

He rose, looked out to sea, and she followed his gaze. The studio had been built as an extension at the rear of the house, windows on all sides. The house was set back from the rocky beach, looking out on the headland stretching to the north, and to the low, straight coast to the south.

There was a jetty down to their right. Tied up was a thirty-foot convertible with a light blue fibreglass hull, a cover tightly drawn over the cockpit. It rocked on the swell, a bell on the small aft mast clanging intermittently. Out to sea there was a lone yacht, puttering on engine power, a tanker, low in the water, in the far distance.

'I don't think I'd be able to write a word if I sat here all day,' he said, then he shook his head. 'Sorry, there I go, making it about me. Tell me about the mosaic.'

She indicated the wicker armchairs by the window, they sat down, their knees close together, and placed their mugs on the small wooden table.

4

The giant squid became her fascination. From *20,000 Leagues Under The Sea,* to articles in National Geographic, she read everything she could find. She studied biology in school, she studied marine zoology at university. It was there, sadly, she discovered that not only did she not have sea legs, but that the sea terrified her. Those long-held fantasies of her as Ahab, searching the seven seas, the career path she had thought of as genuinely plausible, vanished over a long weekend on a small research vessel out of Falmouth. Sunday night, and dry land, could not come quickly enough for her, the last day having been spent curled in a terrified, nauseous ball beneath deck.

* * *

'So the kids started school and I was a bit lost. Michael was away a lot, and I had days when I'd sit at the window back there, before this was built, looking out to sea. Whole days.'

'I'll bet.'

'One day I forced myself out the door. A mosaic class. Just happened to be what was on at the arts centre that week. If it'd been a week later, I don't know, maybe I'd've been quilting a giant squid for the past twelve years, or making Harry Potter figures out of marzipan.'

He laughed, and the sound of it wrapped around her.

'Anyway, for whatever reason, mosaicking clicked.'

'It's absorbing.'

'Yes! I used to do jigsaws when the kids were small.' She smiled at the thought, was going to continue, then shook her head. No one was interested in the inconsequentialities of her parenting life.

'Jigsaws?'

'Will this go in your story? Me and my kids doing jigsaws?'

'Deep background,' he said, smiling.

'You have kids?' she asked.

He held her gaze, and she recognised the defensiveness of the blank stare. He was here to ask the questions.

'The kids and I would do those twenty-piece Winnie-The-

Pooh things with chunky wooden blocks,' she said, before they could slip into awkward silence, 'and then we'd do a fifty-piece, then a hundred. And, of course, it's not rocket science, it's not Mozart composing a symphony, but your kid can do a jigsaw, and you think, wow, you're good at this. Look at the skills!' They both laughed. 'Then suddenly, out of nowhere, you're buying a fifteen-hundred-piece jigsaw of a steam engine, and your kid is excited for two minutes, then frustrated, then bored, and before you know it you're doing it yourself while the kid watches *Thomas*. And I realised one day just how absorbing it was. It stops you thinking. That's the beauty of it. An hour goes by…' and she snapped her fingers. 'But you do a jigsaw and what have you got? Someone else's picture you break up at the end. Then I did the mosaic course, and… there it was, the same feeling of absorption, but at the end of it there was this thing. This thing I'd created. I was hooked. The older the children got, the more time I had.'

'Your husband was supportive?'

A moment, then she looked away, out over the waves. The ever-changing seascape, at once unique and familiar. How did she usually answer that question? With the platitude. With the obvious. He'd paid to have the studio built, so that must mean he'd been supportive.

Except, Michael couldn't have cared less. He had money, too much of it. He had his home by the sea, and his fifteenth floor apartment overlooking the Thames, and his Aston Martin, and his TV legacy cheques, and if she'd asked for ten thousand pounds to fly business to Singapore for a haircut, he'd have obliged. Always happy to substitute money for affection. Or, to equate the two.

'Not really,' she said, the words softly spoken. The truth for once, quickly followed by the realisation she was telling this to a journalist.

'Sorry, I shouldn't say that,' she said. 'Please don't run that.'

'Don't worry. I love the mosaic. This isn't going to be *Husband's Outrage At Triumph of Hero Mosaic Artist*,' making the banner headline as he said it.

She smiled. She felt guilty talking about Michael, yet it was coupled with the sad reflection that it would likely be impossible for her to inspire outrage in him.

'So, what other mosaics have you done? Have you sold at all?'

The straightforward, saving, comfortable question.
She couldn't look at him.

5

At university she met Bryce. Bryce was from Halifax, Nova Scotia, come to Europe to study.

His life goal was to find the giant squid. He would be the first to film an adult, fully healthy, fully grown, giant squid, and it was going to be bigger than anyone imagined. That the natural habitat of such a creature was in the ocean depths was no deterrent. He had his goal, and one day, somewhere in the world, he would achieve it.

That was what brought them together. One day in class, when the squid had been the topic of discussion, they'd more or less taken over, both far more knowledgeable on the subject than the tutor. They had flirted in their competitiveness, and that night they'd gone out, then gone home, and gone to bed.

Bryce had a girlfriend in Halifax, but at first it didn't matter. Not to Alice. She had someone who shared her passion, the relationship was an added bonus.

Then Bryce's aunt in Halifax died, and he had to go home for the funeral. When he returned, having seen the girlfriend and felt the guilt, he broke off with Alice. It was then, when it had been taken away, that she decided she was in love with him.

Yet Bryce and Alice were tied together, and soon enough they were working on a project, and then they were drunkenly making love, then spending weekends down by the sea, or lying in bed, pizza and beer and TV and sex.

All the time, however, the unseen presence of the girlfriend back home. She called three times a week. She wrote love letters. Once the letter included naked pictures. Bryce showed them to Alice.

On and off they went, round and round through three years of university, never ending, never committing. And then university was over. Bryce returned to Halifax and Alice got a job for the summer working as a researcher on a TV production based in Cornwall. A week after he left, Bryce turned up unexpectedly, knocking on Alice's hotel room door at one a.m.

'I've done what I should've done three years ago. Gina and I are through. Come to Halifax with me, babe.'

She said yes. She would move to Canada at the end of the

summer when the TV production was finished.

The following week she met Michael. He had stories to tell, and he was interested in different things. He seemed safe and reliable and when they ended up in bed one night he told her he'd already fallen in love with her. She recognised that there wasn't the same spark she had with Bryce, but that had been a three-year rollercoaster ride, more pain than pleasure, and how could she know he would not now be as capricious with Gina?

She never went to Halifax. She never saw Bryce again. She married Michael.

We live, she'd had many occasions to think, by the choices we make. That was all.

Sometimes she looked for Bryce on the Internet. He was living in Monterey, working for the Bay Aquarium Research Institute, searching for his giant squid in the Monterey Canyon. Married with two children. She contacted him once on Facebook. He never replied.

6

An unplanned dinner at the kitchen table. Quickly thrown-together pasta, a bottle of New Zealand sauvignon blanc.

'What's going to happen to it?' asked Beckett.

He'd spent the hours before asking about every aspect of the mosaic. The symbolism and colours, the sea creatures and the giant squid at the centre of it all. He was more interested in Alice's work, and in Alice herself, than anyone she'd ever met.

All the while, lurking in the shadows, was the thought that she could read nothing into it. He was a journalist. He was literally being paid to be interested.

'I'm not sure. I might try to sell it, maybe give it to a maritime museum.'

'I know some people in Falmouth, at the National. D'you have contacts there?'

'I don't have contacts anywhere.'

'Maybe something'll happen once you've appeared in the paper. You'll get offers.'

You'll get offers.

She closed her eyes on the thought.

'D'you need to earn money from it?'

'No,' she said, 'not really.'

Wouldn't financial independence be nice? To not have to rely, for the rest of her life, on her husband and his disregard?

'If someone buys it,' he said, 'then it disappears, never to be seen in public. If you could come to an arrangement with Falmouth, or County Hall, or North Queensferry perhaps, get the mosaic placed on the ground outside, that would be amazing. It's OK to walk across it?'

She'd spent so many years sitting there, working on the mosaic, that she'd barely thought about what came next. What her life would be once it had been completed. Where the giant squid would go. The achievement, the treasure, was in the journey, not in its completion.

Occasionally she was asked what would happen to it, but the question always seemed framed as a pejorative. A short step from *what are you doing that for?*

'Yes, I guess,' she said. 'If that'd been the intent all along

I'd've likely used a different technique, but this can be adapted. You know, if it's fitted onto a concrete base, tile sealant placed on top. It should be fine.'

'You didn't have a plan when you started?'

He lifted his glass, took a sip. Wine on his moist lips.

Alice, unused to talking about herself, lost in the moment, forcing caution, had no answer other than the truth.

'I couldn't go to sea to search for the squid, so I thought I'd make my own.'

'And why couldn't you search for the squid? If you were a man, you'd think you could rule the world.'

'The sea terrifies me. A small research vessel on a big ocean? The thought of being pitched into the sea, of being beneath the waves…'

'The unknown depths…'

'Exactly. The deep, and what's lurking down there. That's the fascination of the squid, but the thought of diving, or being on the bottom of the ocean in a research submarine, and then coming across one? Oh my goodness.'

She shivered, laughed on the other side.

'That I understand,' he said.

She took a drink, aware that she was drinking faster than him, hoping the flush wouldn't show in her face.

'Regardless, my sea legs are hopeless,' and she giggled. *Giggled?*

He laughed with her. She had begun to allow the thought he was enjoying himself.

'So, even if I wanted to get out there and sail the oceans, my breakfast and I wouldn't be able to leave the port together.'

'You're funny,' he said. 'The boat that's tied down at the jetty there, that's your husband's?'

No one had ever told her she was funny. She held on to that for a moment, then looked at the window. She saw the reflection of the two of them at the table, little more than the rumour of the night outside.

'I love the sound of the bell,' he said. 'It's hypnotic.'

'Yes.'

She'd never talked about the boat. She'd never opened up to anyone. A few hours with Beckett, and he was quickly peeling away the layers of reserve with which she protected herself.

'Michael thought he was being kind. He bought the boat for me, so I could face my fear. Get out there, learn to love being on the water. But it's not a challenge I have any desire to meet. My relationship with the sea will be what it always has been. I'm here, on the shore. It's there, a vast holder of secrets.'

'You never went out on the boat?'

'You know how it is,' she said. 'One must play the part to appease the husband who completely misunderstands you.' *Too much, Alice!* 'I'll go out in a flat calm. And I mean, a *flat* calm. It's not like I have to worry too much about that happening in Caithness.'

He smiled. His eyes flashed understanding, compassion.

She looked away, looked at her plate, wondered if she could drag her fork one last time through the remnants of the sauce. A distraction, cover, to hide the fact she loved the way he made her feel, and the awfulness of the thought that in a day he would be gone, the day after that Michael would return, and two nights from now she'd be sitting in the same position, dinner finished, second glass of wine almost done, the music from *Dances With Wolves* in the background, a deeper silence lingering in the room.

7

She worked on the mosaic late that evening beneath the solitary crane lamp. The head of the squid, the final few pieces to be fitted. Suddenly she wanted to finish it overnight. She wanted Beckett to see it complete when he came back the following day. She wanted to impress him. This thing she had languidly been doing for twelve years, no rush, no commotion, no hurry, no stress, she was now finishing in quixotic fury.

She'd thought of saying he could return when it was done, but it would've been in a few days, and wouldn't that have been absurd? Anyway, Michael would be here, and it would be awkward, and she didn't know how she wouldn't give herself away. Maybe she and Michael had nothing in common. Maybe their relationship was so unromantic it bordered on the formal. But he'd lived with her long enough to see through her, just as she saw through him.

Wheeled nippers in hand, she intricately worked the last few small pieces of tile, cutting them in quarters, shaping them into intricate patterns. The squid flowed, from its arms to its tail, in red and white and pink waves. In the middle of the squid, iridescent jellyfish rose through the water, the rich colours of the squid picked out through the translucent jellyfish shoal.

She placed the last piece of tile not long after midnight. Normally the glue must be left to set, but tonight the wind was at her back, and there was no time. She mixed the grout, applied it to this final panel, a long, slow, patient process, and finished grouting at nine minutes past three.

Just like that, the work of twelve years was over. Not at a canter, but in a foolish, romantic flush. She knelt in the darkness of the night, the light of the lamp trained on the mosaic, laid out as before on the floor, the sound of the waves washing in through the open window, and looked at the giant sea creature she'd brought into creation.

Sadness welled inside her.

* * *

She went to bed at three forty-one. Wide awake, unable to get

Beckett out of her head, she stared at the ceiling, listening to the sound of the sea, as the wind rose and the waves bounced off the rocks.

She could ask him to stay another night. They could have dinner the following evening, they could get gloriously drunk together, then they could fall into bed. It had been so long since she'd had sex, she could barely remember. Over ten years, and then more upon that. Since she'd had sex that made her feel alive, that had inflamed her, had been years beyond counting.

She let her doubts about Beckett float away in the night. Perhaps he showed her the attention because he was being paid to. Perhaps that was his style. Perhaps, perhaps, perhaps. She dismissed it. She was lying alone in bed, the thought of Beckett was warm and wonderful and delicious, and she submitted to it.

8

The wind had picked up through the night, cold from the north, clouds blown in from the sea. Rain in the air.

She felt anxious in a way she hadn't the night before. The evening had been perfect. She needn't have felt she was betraying Michael; thought was not the same as deed. A day all about her, a dinner that had seemed impossibly romantic, though not an amorous word uttered in anger, a few hours' work carried on a magic carpet, and then lying in bed by the light of the night and the sound of the waves.

She woke early, lay still for a short while, unsure of where her mood was, and got up to face the practicalities of the morning. She cleaned her teeth, saving the mouthwash for later. She got in the shower, washed her hair, shaved her legs and armpits. She dried herself, then stood in front of the mirror, looking at her forty-seven year old body.

That wasn't when the doubts kicked in. She didn't need to feel self-conscious. If, as she thought, he felt the same as she did, her body wouldn't matter.

The doubts had started while she was in the shower. The water across her breasts, the razor upon her shin. Was she really going to commit adultery? Was it that straightforward? Would Michael really not care?

The previous night, after Beckett had left, she had felt light. The morning brought uncertainty. Choices to be made, or worse, a choice not even offered. She'd gone to bed worrying about nothing, and had woken in doubt and fear.

And so she could not concentrate on anything; she could only think of Beckett, this man about whom she knew so little. And those thoughts made her feel foolish. A fantasist, carried away on a Mitty-esque flight of the absurd.

She ate breakfast at eight, a piece of toast, a glass of water, two cups of coffee. She sat at the kitchen table, looking out on the grey sea, Radio 3 playing. Breakfast done, she went into the bathroom, checked her teeth for food, then she used the mouthwash. In the mirror her eyes were sad. That was what she always saw, though the previous night they would have sparkled, had she looked.

She returned to the table, poured herself another glass of water. She watched the waves, she vaguely listened to the music. Jean-Marie Leclair, violinist, murdered in his garden in Paris by a hitman paid for by his ex-wife.

Beckett had said he would be over after breakfast, and the night before she hadn't given that any thought. This morning, the vagueness of it haunted her. The entire working day was after breakfast.

Nine o'clock came and went, one radio presenter ticked round to the next. The sky darkened, the view out across the sea became blurry through rain-smeared windows.

Her phone troubled her, the thought of it, of him texting an apology, but it sat silently on the kitchen table, and she determinedly did not look at it.

She made herself a cup of tea, she poured a small bowl of muesli. Nervous, querulous eating, against the grain. The sense of loss formed inside her. A tangible thing she could feel in her throat, in her stomach.

She pushed away the bowl, she lifted the tea, she stood at the kitchen window, clutching the mug, a prop to occupy her mind. The practical Alice, the one she relied upon to see her through every single day, fought to make an appearance, to push aside the Alice who had allowed herself to fall for someone on such slender testimony.

Glances at her phone, willing the doorbell to ring, mug of tea to her lips, tea no longer warm enough, wishing away the minutes.

She lifted her phone, though it refused to ring. The tremble in her fingers annoyed her. She opened the Mail app, and there it was. Second to the top, sandwiched between a twenty per cent sale at John Lewis and a renewal request from the National Trust for Scotland.

The e-mail from Beckett was titled *Sorry*. Like the demolition of a row of apartment blocks, the emotions of the past twenty-four hours crumbled quickly. The hope, the lust, the anticipation, the excitement, the fear.

She couldn't stop herself reading the message.

Called back to London.

Love your story.

I think the mosaic is great.

I got enough to make it work, it'll be a fantastic piece.

I'll arrange for a photographer to visit.

Sorry.

She leant forward on the worktop and stared out of the window. Rain fell, wind blew, waves crested in white. The tumultuous grip of the weather outside mirrored the grip on her insides. The hand wrapped around her stomach, the hope squeezed from her.

She turned away, looked back across the kitchen. She could imagine one of them there, dismissive. Her mother, or Michael. One of the children. Any one of them, asking the question. What had she really thought was going to happen?

She moved quickly, as though there was someone there to walk out on, grabbed a coat off the peg on the back door, threw it on, and headed out into the squall.

9

For a week she fell into a funk. Michael likely noticed upon his return, but said little. One night he asked if everything was all right, but the conventions of the marriage demanded that she insist that it was, and that he inquire no further. That was who they were. He was not interested in any case. Five days after he returned, talking vaguely of an unnamed project he would likely never write, he said he had to be in London, and possibly New York, and left again the following day.

For days Alice looked out on the sea, standing at the kitchen window, or sitting on the rocks. Talking to herself, lessons from her more practical half.

'You weren't going to sleep with him anyway,' she said. The sky was light blue, the clouds sparse and high, wind blew from the land, the sea like corrugated iron. 'The wife, the part you play, would have kicked in. Guilt would've had its say.'

That's what she said, as she sat on a rock, her coat tight around her on a chill day, her elbow on her knee, her chin in the palm of her hand. For the first time in a week she imagined a squid washing up on the rocks.

* * *

One evening, while Michael was away, she allowed herself to celebrate the completion of the mosaic. Beckett had walked into her life, had disrupted it, and then he'd walked back out again. It was eleven days before finally she could take some pleasure in the culmination of twelve years work.

Bombay Sapphire, Fever Tree, a slice of lemon, a large glass, lots of ice. Crisp, sharp, fresh. She toasted herself, standing in the studio, looking down on her creation. Too early to feel any joy at the work completed, too early to feel deflated, too early to wonder what she would do next.

The photographer had yet to come. Maybe he never would. Maybe the article would never happen. That awful morning, waiting for the doorbell to ring, still sat uncomfortably in the pit of her stomach. Eleven days, and still the doorbell hadn't rung.

The doorbell rang.

She looked out across the sea, the sky dark on the horizon, night closing in from the east. She took a drink, felt the cold of the ice against her lips, the tonic sharp in her mouth, the lemon bitter on her tongue, the alcohol biting the back of her throat.

This is how stories are told, she thought. This is how we come to where we are. A creature on a beach. A lifelong obsession. Two people, neither comfortable with the force of attraction. And then, at some inexplicable, perfect moment, the doorbell rings.

She downed the gin and tonic. Three-quarters of the glass. Took a last look over the sea, then walked to the front of the house.

There was a woman in a suit, white blouse tight around her neck, immaculate make-up, early thirties.

'Hey, Alice?' she said. American. 'You're Alice?'

'Yes.'

'Great. Sorry to doorstep you like this. I meant to call on the way.' She held forward her business card, which she seemed to produce in a flowing movement from some part of her suit that didn't have any pockets. 'Katie Warren, I'm from The National Aquarium in Falmouth. I've been talking to the arts correspondent at the Times. We've been looking for a centrepiece outside the building. We're right in the heart of the port. Great location.'

'I know it,' said Alice. Her voice sounded distant, as though someone else had spoken.

'Great. They showed me some pictures, and I have to say, your work looks incredible. Sorry I didn't call to set up the meeting. Meant to do it on the way, then I got tied up with a call to Florida, and then there was a thing with my OB-GYN – you do not want to know about that…' She smiled. 'And then there was another thing with a guy named Larry, you know how it is, and suddenly I'm here.'

The flurry of words came to an end. She looked earnestly at Alice. 'Is this a good time?'

And this is how stories are told.

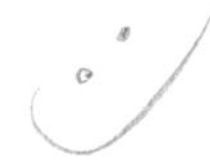

Six Months Later

A small opening ceremony in Falmouth. A cold, grey day, mist out on the sound, and beyond. Three days earlier, in the Saturday lifestyle section, timed to tie in with that week's unveiling, Beckett's piece in the Times.

Michael read it. 'You should've had your hair done for the picture,' he said. That was all.

Her mum called, there were other messages. People who had never been particularly curious, were now delighted to discover the mosaic was a work of art, praised by experts. It had been validated. Rather than a curiosity, it was something to be approved of.

There were three journalists and two photographers. A junior member of the Royal family, with a remit for the oceans, unveiled the mosaic, the small crowd of bystanders applauded. A speech from Katie Warren, a few words from Alice, and then the unveiling party retreated to a room in the aquarium.

There Alice stood, a glass of Prosecco in hand, beside a blue green tank filled with small, exotic fish. She had been the centre of attention for a short while, but the junior royal had remained for the drinks and canapés, and Alice was forgotten.

Uncomfortable in the cocktail setting, she was happy to have an activity. Looking at fish, her back turned on the party. Attuned to his voice, she could hear Michael talking. Holding court on the subject of his hit one-off nineties show with a young Simon Pegg.

She'd hoped Beckett would be there, although they had exchanged a few e-mails over the months, and she knew he couldn't make it. At some point along the way she'd adjusted. Their day together had grown in significance, but had been filed away. The romance that never happened; the chance that slipped through her fingers; the best sex she ever had, but really never had. The beautiful, perfect melancholy of lost love.

Two clown fish harmoniously changing direction, several goldfish and a dwarf cichlid, the languid movement of a blue shrimp on the floor of the tank.

'It looks good.'

Her stomach thundered into her mouth. Her heart... *oh, her heart!*

'The mosaic in that position,' said Beckett. 'It's perfect.'

She had to swallow before speaking, then managed to say, 'Thank you.'

'There must be a big empty space in your studio.'

'There is.'

She had to swallow again, this time Prosecco. A long drink.

'Are you working on something new?'

Another drink.

'I thought I'd take my time. Didn't want to rush into it.'

He smiled. 'The difficult second album.'

'Yes.'

She finished the glass, she finally managed to look at him. She held his gaze for no more than a second, then turned quickly back to the fish. She felt naked, every emotion on display.

In some vague, distant part of the room she could hear Michael. The unbroken, amusing monologue.

'I'm sorry. I...' Beckett's apology began, but, whatever it was to be, it could not be formed.

'Did you have a good reason?' she asked. Her heart at a clip.

There was no one standing close to them. The mosaic had been unveiled, her creation had been unleashed, they were finished with her.

'Yes.'

'Then you don't have to explain. We all have stories to tell.'

Eyes lowered, she searched for Michael's voice, finding it in the same place.

She thought of random words from conversations she'd had in her head these past few months. All those days walking the coast, up to the headland, down on to the beach, trying to think of her next project, thinking mostly of Beckett. Torn between longing, regret, and giving in to the fantasy.

'I still hear the bell,' he said. His voice had softened. A faraway sound, lying in a bed, the window open, the sound of the sea and the clank of a lanyard, and the bell on a boat in a swell. 'That's how I ground my thoughts of you. The rhythmic clang of the bell, the waves on the rocks. And the sound of your voice. I was asking all those questions. You were probably thinking I was doing my job. But I wanted to hear you talk. I wanted to know everything about you.'

She watched a diamond blue discus weave through the slowly swaying fronds of a fern. She didn't want him to stop talking.

'I still do,' he said, voice seemingly even more distant. 'And here I am'

The softly spoken words drifted away, consumed by the sounds of the room. The hum of the fish tanks, the low level of chatter, the higher voice of a woman standing a few yards away, regurgitating a conversation about the Tate.

'The reason you didn't come back the next day?' she asked. 'That still exists?'

Alice wanted to hold his hand, take his fingers into hers, linger over the touch.

She noticed a gap in the fabric of sound. What had happened to Michael's voice, the drone to which she had fixed his whereabouts?

'Alice.'

She jumped at his touch, turned, her eyes widening briefly, before regaining control.

'Sorry,' she said.

'You all right?'

'Yes, just got lost. It's hypnotic.'

She indicated the tank. Michael looked at Beckett. Nevertheless, he wasn't one to spend time on what he didn't understand.

'Look, sorry, we're going to have to run. Tomorrow's meeting in London just got bumped to this evening, if you can believe it. We have to be on the three-fifteen from Truro.' He looked at his watch.

They had a room booked in Falmouth, seats on the Cornish Riviera Express the following morning at eight. Breakfast in the dining car.

They'd made so many journeys on the back of his job over the years, and she'd played her part. Now they'd come the length of the country for her, the culmination of twelve years work, and he wanted to leave. Something he was involved in that would never happen was more important than something she'd achieved. Usually she would've been hurt. Angry. Even in this soulless marriage, in which romance never played a part, where intimacy was subordinate to function, it would have riled her. Now, she didn't care. *How she didn't care!*

'You don't have to come,' he said, the words an afterthought, it only just occurring to him that she might not want to.

'I'd like to stay,' she said. 'I'll see you in London tomorrow.

I'll text when I get in.'

Michael glanced quickly at Beckett, then looked around. He seemed to be searching for something else to say, and then he touched her arm. 'Have a nice afternoon.'

He kissed her cheek, didn't look at Beckett, and left. She watched him for a moment, before resuming the position. Just her, and Beckett, and the fish in the tank.

More time passed. The clown fish swam through the ferns, an anemone pulsed in the movement of the water. The awkwardness of the moment hung in the air a little longer than Michael, but slowly it began to lift.

Now I can touch your hand, she thought.

She turned, looked again around the room. It was almost clear. The junior member of the Royal Family had left, the flow of Prosecco had stopped, any reason to linger had been removed. There was no sign of Katie Warren, having escorted the royal from the premises before returning to work.

No one cares about the mosaicist. Not the way they care about the painter and the sculptor. The mosaic becomes part of the fabric of the floor or the wall or the street or the building, while the mosaicist herself is forgotten. The ceremony, small as it was, hadn't been about her.

They stood in silence. At last she touched his fingers, having braced herself for the electricity of it.

'Come on,' she said.

They walked out the aquarium, across the mosaic of the giant squid, leaving it behind.

* * *

A blind had been drawn across the window on the world, the mist had rolled in from the sea. They walked out on the pier from where the small passenger ferries left for Flushing and St Mawes. The sea was engulfed, the town was quiet, the air cold.

From the end of the pier they could barely see twenty yards across the water. Two orange buoys moved slowly with the swell. To the left, one of the ferries butted gently against the side of the pier. No crew, no passengers, no chance of sailing. Occasionally, in the back and forth of the swell, the bell on the boat clanged.

They leant on the railing, where sometimes seagulls perched. Small waves splashed up against the pier wall beneath their feet.

Out on the water, lost in the wall of mist, a motorboat puttered slowly away from shore.

This was the same mist as the one that had brought the squid in the first place. Wherever it had been all these years, it was back now, at the end of her story. The young squid had come to her, washed up on the shore. Now, fully formed, the squid of her creation had been released from her keeping, off to find its place in a fogbound world.

She thought of the boy on the beach, and how she had wondered if he'd ever really existed. And now she imagined she could turn and Beckett would be gone, because he had never really existed either. His part in the narrative had been completed. It hadn't been about lust or compassion, just a plot device to round out the circle, find somewhere for her squid to belong.

'The fog's so thick,' he said, the sound of his voice liquid. 'Feels like we could melt into it.'

Their hands were still touching, their fingers linked. Their arms came closer together until they pressed against each other.

There was a flutter of noise through the mist, a gull landed on the railing. It cocked its head to the side, watched them for a moment, then turned and looked back up the pier, the little that could be seen of it.

Soon enough, the gull was just a thing that was there, immovable as the pier and the mist and the railings. Beckett lightly ran his fingers down her cheek, and when she faced him he leaned forward and softly pressed his lips against hers.

Aged forty-seven, Alice on the pier, lost in the fog.

Iron Man

(A DI Westphall Story)

A day in late October.

It began like any other. Alarm clock and a shower, coffee and eggs and the news on the radio, the short drive through town, e-mails and paperwork. Now I've been called to a house on the hill above Marybank. Standing on the doorstep, back turned to the door, there's a beautiful view down over the glen, across to Ben Wyvis. Today the sun is shining, the sky a perfect blue. The air is still, the smell of a wood-burning stove lingers in the morning.

The door opens, and I turn, my ID card already in hand.

'Mrs Murray?'

The woman – mid-fifties, her face creased with worry – glances at the card, then steps back without speaking. She knows I have not come with further bad news, yet my arrival adds another layer to the drama, another tick in the box of reality. Detective Inspectors don't come to houses in the middle of the morning for nothing. There will be no one to pinch her to wake her from this nightmare.

Into the house, the front door closing behind me, and we walk together through to the kitchen. Here is Constable Fisher, and a man dressed in anxiety. On the table, two pieces of toast gone cold in the rack, a half-eaten bowl of muesli, a forgotten jug of milk. An abandoned breakfast, a failed clutch at normality. Outside, a small back garden, a child's brightly coloured plastic tricycle discarded on the lawn.

'Constable,' I say, with a nod at Fisher to begin. The story will come more quickly from her.

'Sir. Jason is five and lives here with his grandparents. He went to bed at seven-thirty last night, as usual. Mrs Murray checked on him at eleven. All seemed well. He'd obviously been reading for a while, and had fallen asleep with the book on his bed. Jason usually wakes first thing, at around six…'

'He's our alarm clock,' says Mr Murray. Staring at the floor.

'Cock-a-doodle-do,' says his wife.

Funny words, sadly escaping into the room, swallowed by fear.

'Mr Murray woke at just after eight,' continues Fisher, 'and was instantly worried.'

'First thing I thought of,' interjects Murray. 'The very first thing.'

'He went through to Jason's room. Jason wasn't there. He searched the house, and there was no sign.' Fisher glances out of the window, nodding towards the garden. 'Same.'

'You've spoken to the neighbours?'

'Yes,' says Fisher. 'On either side, and several houses across the road. No one saw or heard anything. In any case, the doors are locked and bolted from the inside.'

'Windows?'

'All locked from the inside. It's impossible to see how Jason could have left the house.'

We share a glance. The acknowledgement between us that we're likely standing in a room with at least one person who's not telling the truth.

'Does Jason like hide and seek?' I ask, directing the question to Mr Murray.

'He loves it,' he replies. 'But we've searched every hiding place he knows.' He waves an indifferent arm. 'There aren't that many places he could be.'

Defiant, he glances at his wife. I give him the space to talk, though it is Mrs Murray who fills it.

'Someone must have broken in,' she says. 'I don't know how they got out and made it look like the doors were locked, but they must have. What other explanation could there be?'

I turn to her, but she's not looking at me. She's staring at the floor. Hard to tell where those words came from, but they were forced. Desperate to believe them, or desperate to find an alternative to what she already knows.

'I'm going to look at the back garden,' I say. 'Walk with me, Constable. I'll just be a moment,' I add to the grandparents.

We go out into the back, stepping up to the rear of the property. Turning back to the house, Strathconon stretches away to our left, ahead in the distance the green slopes of Wyvis. The day, perfect and clear, is juxtaposed with the stifling fear and guilt of the kitchen.

'You think the boy's hiding?' asks Fisher. 'Or dead?'

'One of them's lying. So, yes, either he has a hiding place they don't know about, or...'

'It's a small house.'

'It is.'

It's obvious which of the two options is more likely, the seeming inevitability of it left unsaid.

'Who's your money on?' asks Constable Fisher.

'Too early to say. Let's split them up. You talk to Mrs Murray, I'll get grandpa to show me the boy's bedroom.'

'Sir.'

We head back inside, leaving behind the pure, still day, the cry of a gull. Into the kitchen, where the players still stand in silence, Mrs Murray now with a cup of cold tea unthinkingly in her hand.

I nod at the grandfather and say, 'Can you show me Jason's room, please?'

He and his wife are both close to being unable to function, but he looks more likely to bludgeon his way through the day with forced practicality.

'Of course,' he says.

We go into the hall, and up the stairs. Beige carpet, magnolia walls, a print of the Glenfinnan viaduct, another of an East Neuk fishing harbour. Behind me, Fisher starts talking, her voice low.

We come to the top of the stairs, past the bathroom, and into the small bedroom at the end.

I feel it as soon as I walk through the door. Indeed, I could feel it out in the corridor, as though the atmosphere of what happens in this room was reaching out beyond its confines, across the portal, trying to escape. Or looking to be rescued.

It is a five-year-old's room like any other. Blue walls, white ceiling. Toys littering the carpet. Iron Man and Thor on the bed, three *Avengers* posters on the wall, a Spiderman outfit dumped on the floor.

Mr Murray walks into the room ahead of me, and stops. He looks around, his head drops.

'I could weep,' he says.

I don't doubt that he could.

My eyes are immediately drawn to the far corner on the left. There is a wardrobe against the front wall of the house, and then a space of a couple of feet between the sidewall and the wardrobe.

I stare into the space, trying to understand. What is in the space does not make any sense, but it does at least tie in with the feeling in the room.

The grandfather sees that I am distracted. He follows my gaze into the corner. He does not see what I see.

'What?' he asks.

'Where are Jason's parents?'

I turn away from the gap between the wardrobe and the wall.

The gap in reality.

Mr Murray seems reluctant to answer. Finally, with a shake of the head, 'We don't know who his dad is. His mum couldn't cope. She's in Durness.'

'How often does Jason see her?'

The words, 'Every couple of months,' are squeezed into the room.

That is all. He's looking at me, wondering what else is to come, but I have nothing else to ask him. I have everything I need.

I do not look back to the gap between the wardrobe and the wall.

We return downstairs. Constable Fisher and Mrs Murray are in the kitchen, Mrs Murray crying.

* * *

'She thinks her husband might have killed him and hidden the body,' says Fisher.

We stand once more in the garden, eyes on Mr and Mrs Murray in the kitchen. They talk in low voices, their lips barely moving.

'Is there a history of violence? Sexual abuse?' I ask.

'She wouldn't say. I'm not getting the full story.'

'What about the daughter?'

'She's always been dominated by her dad. He didn't give her the option of looking after Jason. She was a teenage mother, wasn't sure who the father was, and her dad basically took control and banished her.'

'OK. Can you call Child Protection?'

'Don't we need to find the boy first?'

A pause. The sky is the same unbelievable blue, there is still wood smoke in the air.

Constable Fisher is a practical woman, and this transcends rationality.

'This'll take a delicate touch, Constable,' I say. 'We need to break the spell of the house. For now we'll take Mr Murray into custody, let his wife think we know more than we do, and hope it inspires her to open up. And we need to get their daughter back here. She should be with her son.'

'But the boy?'

I gesture to the upstairs of the house, albeit we cannot see

Jason's window from where we are.

'He's standing in the corner of the bedroom.'

A beat. I'm not looking at her, but I can feel Fisher's curious eyes.

'Really?'

'I held his gaze,' I say. 'He lifted his forefinger to his lips.'

'Why didn't Mr Murray see him?'

Another beat. Here is the notion that crosses the line from irrationality into impossibility.

'Jason has learned to make himself invisible.'

The pragmatist in Fisher does not let her move away. She will feel she needs more of an explanation before she can act on this, yet there is not too much more that can be said.

'How could *you* see him?' she asks.

'Maybe he wanted me to. Maybe I can see things others can't. You'll see him now you know he's there.'

'That's...' she begins, but her words are lost.

'Go and get him, Constable,' I say, turning now. 'I'll call it in. We'll need another car out here to take Mr Murray to the station. It should be a long time before Jason sees his grandfather again.'

* * *

Driving into Dingwall, an officer from Child Protection beside me. In the back of the car sits Jason Murray. He is staring out of the window, an Iron Man figure in his hands.

We turn right onto the A835, the last of the autumn leaves bright yellow in the early afternoon sun. A convoy of cars pass in the other direction, stuck behind a tractor. Above, contrails cross in the sky, crows fly in angry, tight circles. Jason holds Iron Man close to his chest.

The Tarantino Version

She was late again. Third night that week. Henry Cole had given up looking at the clock.

He sat at the dining room table, his dinner plate long since cleared away, now with papers in neat piles around him. Ray Charles was playing on low volume, but the atmosphere of the room was dictated by the harsh glare of the central ceiling light.

For Cole it was just another night, home alone, marking school essays. As ever, the standard had noticeably dropped since the previous year, yet he was beholden to give even more As and Bs. Even those who could barely understand sentence structure were required to be given at least a C.

He was unsure what to do with the essay from Teagan Bates, which had consisted of the line *Mistuh Cole your a fuckin wanker* written three hundred times. It was entitled, 'Repetition'. Perhaps he could dock her marks for missing the apostrophe in *you're*.

The front door opened. Cole closed his eyes for a second, his head still lowered over the table, then he turned slowly and looked into the hallway.

Their eyes met. Her look was of contempt; in return, his was one of browbeaten, abject poverty of spirit. For several seconds she stood and stared at him, then finally she sneered, walked quickly out of his line of vision, and up the stairs. Shortly afterwards he heard the shower running.

* * *

He was talking about Stalin. No one in the Year 9 history class seemed particularly interested. They were chatting, texting, watching YouTube. He'd never had the balls to take a phone from a pupil. One of his fellow teachers had. Later that day the kid's father had arrived, kneecapped the teacher with a baseball bat, and extracted an apology from the headmaster. Those were the kinds of things that happened, and no one seemed to care anymore.

* * *

That evening he was supposed to attend a teachers' dinner, but decided not to. He had no more to say to most of them than he did to Janey. He'd paid for his ticket, but the money didn't bother him. Most teachers' dinners he would have happily paid not to go to anyway.

He came home early. He'd assumed Janey wouldn't be there, but instead he found her banging Rupert on the sofa. Lying back, legs in the air, the dress Henry had bought her three Christmases ago bunched at her waist, her bra tossed to the other side of the room, Rupert thrusting into her with his massive cock.

Henry had never seen Rupert's cock, he just assumed it was massive.

She caught Henry's eye over Rupert's shoulder and seemed annoyed.

Henry watched for a few moments, and then left the room.

He had a gun. An old gun, which he kept under the bed. His father had somehow hung onto it when he'd completed his National Service. It had never been discharged, but Henry had a couple of bullets.

He wasn't sure what came over him, but he started the process without thinking. Up the stairs, into the spare room, down on his knees, rummaging around in all the things crammed beneath the bed until he found the old shoebox, faded red.

He weighed the gun in his hand. He felt nothing. He aimed it at himself in the dusty mirror, looking down the sight. He had no clear thought on how this was going to play out, no sudden strengthening of his resolve, no hatred, no bile. He had a gun in his hand, that was all, and at that moment his wife was having sex with another man.

Henry walked into the sitting room with the gun, just as Rupert was slamming Janey with his huge cock from behind. Rupert stopped and looked over his shoulder. Lowering her head, Janey looked back at Henry through the gap in her sagging breasts. Henry was pointing the gun.

'What the fuck?' said Rupert.

He disengaged, walked over to Henry, took the gun from him and tossed it casually onto the other sofa.

'Now, if you don't mind fucking off,' he said.

Henry was looking at Rupert's cock, which wasn't so huge after all.

* * *

Henry wandered through town, feeling pathetic. He stopped to buy a sandwich in Subway, although he didn't sit in. He didn't usually go out in the evenings. A lot of people seemed drunk although it was only 6.45pm. He passed the local cinema, which was showing a Tarantino retrospective. He'd never heard of Tarantino. The rain had just begun, and he was wondering what to do until Rupert had gone. There was a film starting in five minutes. On the poster a woman with black hair, lying on her stomach, looked out at him from behind her cigarette, her legs crossed in the air behind her. Her low neckline revealed the top of her breasts. Henry felt a strange feeling in his throat and went inside.

He left ninety minutes later. Not because he wasn't enjoying it, but because he wanted to get home before Rupert left. Somewhere in amongst the Royale with Cheese, and the gold watch, and the foot massage, and the *check the big brain on Brett*, he had found his balls.

His motherfucking balls.

* * *

When the door opened they were sitting naked together on the sofa watching a repeat of *Deal Or No Deal*. They probably weren't going to have sex again, they just hadn't bothered getting dressed. Rupert's cock looked insignificant. He yawned. Janey joined him.

'What?' said Rupert.

The gun was where Rupert had left it. Henry picked it up and stood in front of them. Rupert noticed something different about him and shifted slightly. Janey raised an eyebrow.

'Get the fuck out of my house,' said Henry.

'This is… ' began Rupert, but the words quickly dried up.

Henry, face set hard, let a grim silence settle upon the room.

Rupert swallowed.

'Get the fuck,' repeated Henry slowly, 'out of my house.'

Rupert's cock was shriveling into nothingness. Rupert could tell that Henry had found his balls, and didn't like it.

Janey, on the other hand, was made of harder stuff.

'Henry' she said, dismissively, 'go and make yourself a cup of Ovaltine, and go to bed.'

'You will know I am the Lord,' said Henry, ignoring Janey, 'when I lay my vengeance upon you.'

'You're the what?' said Rupert.

Rupert was beginning to panic.

'Get the fuck away from my motherfucking wife!' said Henry.

'Oh, for crying out loud, Henry, have you been watching *Scooby Doo* again? Put it away. And for your information, I have never fucked anyone's mother. Now, piss off.'

For some reason Rupert held up a cushion in self-defence. Henry grabbed it, thrust it against the end of the gun and shot them both in the face. The cushion barely muffled the sound of the gunfire, of course, but the neighbours, all sat in front of Sky Sports and BBC3 and ITV2 watching overpaid cheating footballers, and Stacey and Jimbo and Charlene, and mums whose daughters sleep with their best friend's dad, and daughters whose mums sleep with their best friend's son, heard nothing.

Henry studied the corpses of his wife and her lover for a while. There was blood and brain matter all over the sofa and the wall behind.

'This is some fucked-up, repugnant shit,' he said quietly to himself.

He made a plan, and then he efficiently cleaned up the mess for all the world like he was being directed by The Wolf.

Then he disposed of the bodies, and ate supper.

* * *

The pupils were noisy. They hadn't noticed Henry's new balls. He gave them a couple of minutes and then picked up the baseball bat he'd brought into class. No one noticed a baseball bat in school anymore. With one flowing movement he raised it, then brought it smashing down onto the edge of his desk.

The walls shook. There was quiet.

'Now all of you just shut... the fuck... up.'

There was a moment of silence. Several of the pupils had to stop themselves laughing nervously.

'Let's talk about Stalin,' said Henry.

'What?' said one boy at the back, his tone somewhere between awe and fear.

'Stalin,' said Henry, 'was one badass motherfucker. Now open you books at page fifty-nine.'

No one moved.

'What?' said the same kid, as though he'd been silently elected nervous spokesperson for the class.

'Say 'what' again,' said Henry, looking at the kid. 'I dare you. I double-dare you, motherfucker. Say 'what' one more, Goddam, time.'

He held the boy's gaze. The boy wilted.

Henry looked over the class. They had all wilted. They were all in awe of Henry's new balls.

And no one said 'what'.

Henry waited another few moments, then slowly rested the bat against the edge of the desk.

'Now, pretty please, with sugar on top, open the fucking books.'

Twenty-three pupils opened twenty-three books, and by the end of the lesson, each one of them had learned that yes, Stalin was indeed a badass motherfucker.

One More Cup
Of Coffee

1

She held the compass lightly in her fingers for the last time. It was barely more than an inch across, manufactured in 1879 by Francis Barker & Sons, London. Blued steel needle with gold letters, pivoting above a sunburst dial.

She placed the folded piece of paper on top of the glass, clipped the brass lid back into place, and laid the compass on the bench. She let her fingers rest on it for another few seconds, and then abruptly stood.

'We should go,' she said to the girl, who was playing at the side of a fountain.

The girl pointed at the bench.

'Mummy, you left your box.'

Marianna took the girl's hand and found that she could not speak. They walked quickly down Avenue Gardens and out of Regent's Park.

Marianna had been drinking in the same small café for five years, ever since she'd arrived in London. Close to Charing Cross Road, but far enough away and round a corner so that the tourists never came; near to St Giles-in-the-Fields, where the drunks and the addicts were, though none of them paid her much attention. They sensed her melancholy, fearing it might be infectious.

She loved the café for its simplicity. Coffee and tea, croissants and pain au chocolat. A Parisian chic she imagined, although she had never been to Paris. Every morning she found herself spending at least half an hour longer than she intended; and her own shop would be opened half an hour late.

One Monday morning, in the spring of 2009, she arrived slightly earlier than usual. The café had been redecorated, the furniture replaced. There was a menu board behind the counter offering flat white, latte and decaf. The two members of staff wore the same uniform. A small piece of card on each table promised WiFi.

Marianna removed her earphones, as she usually did on arriving at the shop now, and studied the new layout. So different from before, it confused her. She looked for Elyot, but he wasn't there, and she instantly assumed he had gone with the makeover. Making a hurried and slightly panicked decision, she turned and walked out.

Elyot returned from the kitchen eleven seconds later. He checked to see if Marianna was there, but she wasn't due for another ten or fifteen minutes. He felt the draught of cold air, of someone having just left the shop, but the same customers were in as had been a few minutes earlier.

One of them caught Elyot's eye. Elyot nodded and walked over to her table.

* * *

For years Marianna never knew why her mother hated her, then suddenly one day it seemed obvious and she felt stupid for not having realised. She could have hated her mother in return, but felt nothing. Instead, she went home, packed a bag and left.

Her grandparents had been caught up in the persecution at the start of the war. They had hidden for a while, pretended to be people they weren't, a religion they weren't. They hadn't liked denying their culture, but the young Jacob Zieliński had recognised the danger. Eventually they had been betrayed, and the young couple had been taken from the outskirts of Gdańsk and sent to the camps. However, they had managed to leave Marianna's father with a neighbour, a baby born into tragedy.

Always strong enough to work, Jacob had gone from Stutthof to Majdanek to Auschwitz, somehow surviving the final death march to Buchenwald, to be liberated by the Americans. He had returned to Gdańsk, where his son waited for the stranger to come home. Jacob's wife never saw Gdańsk again, an early victim of the gassing vans in Chelmno.

Jacob, having escaped the persecution of the Nazis, did not escape the persecution of his fellow Poles. He never did get his son back, he never did get to live the miserable, austere life of his fellow countrymen under the Soviets.

Back in Gdańsk, they asked how he had survived. When so many had died, how was it possible that Jacob Zieliński had seen out the war? Some screamed *kolaborator!* Jacob was hounded; hounded and killed. Marianna's father grew up with strangers, the Jew in him was lost.

He moved to Warsaw when he was eighteen.

* * *

Elyot waited all morning. Slowly he came to realise what must have happened. Marianna had arrived while he'd been in the kitchen; the place had changed, the other two waiters were new, her equilibrium had been lost, she had turned round and walked out.

If only Harrison had been there he could have said something to Marianna, or at least to Elyot when he'd returned. But Harrison was gone, too old for the modern coffee shop, and the two waiters in uniformed attendance had not known the woman who sat every morning with her coffee, reading *Gazeta Wyborcza.*

Marianna had never spoken to Elyot. She would listen, and sometimes smile. He presumed that she didn't speak English, or was embarrassed to speak it. Maybe she didn't speak at all. They had enjoyed the spirit of it, the one-way conversations every weekday morning. The longing had gone unspoken, but in other ways Elyot had found his voice. And Marianna felt that he understood her, and that in some peculiar way she had gone beyond speech.

By the end of that week, realization had settled upon him and he felt sure she would not be back. Friday evening at six o'clock, Elyot removed his new uniform and resigned. The following Monday morning he returned to Charing Cross Road and began methodically searching other coffee houses in the area; plain coffee houses with neither latte nor WiFi. There weren't many.

Four times that day Elyot walked past Marianna's shop, yet he never noticed her. She catered to a niche market, and had no reason to try to tempt in the random passerby.

Each time Elyot walked past her invisible shop front, she was sitting at the back in her small workshop area, her head down over a Georgian gimbaled marine compass, dating from the 1820s. The pointer was missing, but she had spares of the right size and vintage. The dry card was pristine, thirty-two cardinal and inter-cardinal points, a large *Fleur de lis* for North. The mahogany bowl was slightly damaged, the brass gimbal dented. She would repair the imperfections. She was in no hurry. Business wasn't good, but it was adequate. Over time, the right people had come to know her, and to trust her work.

For now, however, Elyot passed it all by.

2

The compass was picked up ten minutes later by a small boy. He didn't even try to open it. Maybe he didn't realise that it could be opened. He hit it a couple of times, and then threw it into the grass.

Marianna's father arrived in Warsaw in 1957. The city had been rebuilt, the Palace of Culture & Science was temporarily the tallest building in Europe, and Poland was beholden to the Soviet Union. He got a job working in construction. Life was hard. Many years later he met and married Ania Rutkowska. She was twelve years younger than him. He thought they would have children, but nothing happened for a very long time. They had their moments of light, but generally they had given up, they were unhappy, and they lived their bleak life among people who queued for food and had never recovered.

When Ania fell pregnant it was the first time they had made love in two and a half years, a vodka-fuelled fumble on the sofa which Ania would have called rape had she wanted to call it anything. Marianna was born on a beautifully warm June morning in 1985. Her father celebrated in drink.

He worked on building sites, Marianna's mother brought up the baby and had her husband's dinner on the table at the required time.

One snowy night in December 1993, when the city of Warsaw was quiet, her father came to Marianna's bedroom for the first time. She was eight and a half. He called it their secret. Somehow the word stuck. Even after puberty, even when she was a more enlightened teenager, she still thought of it as their secret.

* * *

Elyot had only known Marianna for six months, and even at that it was a stretch to say that he'd known her at all. But once she was gone, London seemed tired. He saw the same faces in amongst the millions. He had done the galleries, he had walked the Mall and the royal parks, he had seen the shows, he had embraced the city, its size and its diversity. Yet, suddenly, without the presence of this woman who had never spoken a word to him, it seemed empty, bereft of life.

He took a job as a researcher in maritime history at the University of Bath. It didn't pay much, and there he was, not long turned twenty-eight, living in amongst students, being drawn into their lives, still listening to Dylan, converting as many as he could. He soon found himself in a relationship with a nineteen year-old Chinese mathematics student; frantic, exciting sex, and strange boredom he didn't understand.

* * *

Marianna was working on an old 3" box compass that she'd picked up on a trip to Massachusetts. She could tell the man was watching her, but she generally didn't engage the customers unless they gave her no choice. It would have been preferable to work behind a door with no shop front, but her accountant had told her often enough that she had to take all the business she could get.

Blood On The Tracks was playing in the background. Some people mentioned the music when they entered, but not this man.

'What's that you're working on?' he asked.

She didn't look up. The conversation would be forced. She had lost the art of it the day she had realised why her mother hated her. The day she'd realised that the secret she shared with her father wasn't a secret.

Her mother hadn't confronted her, hadn't walked in on them, there had been no uncomfortable family revelation. Marianna had been sitting in a small café on Aleje Jerozolimskie near the center of town, nursing a slow cup of coffee, watching the cars. From nowhere, suddenly it was obvious. Her mother had known all along. She could not begin to fathom why she had not said anything, why she had thought so little of her daughter that she had not put a stop to it, but at that moment she knew why her mother hated her.

She went home, she packed a bag. Her father was still at the factory, her mother was in the kitchen chopping vegetables. Marianna stood in the doorway for a few seconds, coat on, her bag in her hand. Her mother stared blankly. '*Wyjeżdżam*,' Marianna said. Her mother did not reply.

You let this happen to me all these years.

– *You stole my husband.*

She turned and walked quickly from the house. She neither saw nor heard from her mother again. That night her father was distraught. The next morning found him dead in blood-red bathwater.

The man in the shop was named Burke. He looked like her father. But then, so did everyone.

'It is a Wilcox Crittenden,' she said. She caught his eye, but only briefly. 'Early 1920s. If you have heard the name, it is probably because of their toilets.'

'They make toilets?'

'Marine toilets.'

'What do you do, exactly?'

She looked up, curious why he continued to make an effort. He smiled. He had dimples, white teeth. His eyes smiled too. She might have wondered if she knew him, but she didn't know anybody.

'I...,' she began, unsure whether he was actually interested, 'it depends. Sometimes, if the piece works, I do not like to do anything. Some customers want the wear and tear, they want the compass to look as if it has been around the world.'

'I like that,' he said. 'A salty old relic that's sailed the seven seas. It's seen action on the Spanish Main, and once went down in the Baltic with a Russian cargo vessel, before washing up on the Suffolk coast.'

She continued, not wanting to be swept up by the romance of his voice. 'Sometimes, if the piece is obviously not working, if the needle needs replaced, or the fluid, if the card is missing, I will repair that.' She talked quickly, drily, not allowing him to interrupt. 'Although you want the piece to retain as much of its original detail as possible.'

She looked up, expecting him to still be staring at her. He was holding a Sherwood & Co. WW1 military pocket watch compass. It was in pristine condition. She'd liked the simplicity of it, the military arrow denoting that it was War Department issue.

'This, for example,' he said, 'much too clean.'

Such assurance in speech.

3

The compass lay in the grass for a few days. No one noticed it, no one stepped on it. Some time later, a lawn mower swept past, no more than six inches away. About to swing the mower around, the Gardener saw the brass, dull in amongst the grass. He bent down, inspected the small box, slipped it into his pocket and forgot about it.

Burke was amused by Marianna's discomfort, had her down as borderline Asperger's. The lower end of the scale, largely manifesting itself in a general discomfort with other people. Which explained why she so rarely met his eye. However, he had managed to progress beyond the conversation on compasses, to tempt her away from her workshop and away from her one-bedroomed flat off the King's Road.

He had chosen the wine and the food without looking at the menu.

'You're a tough nut to crack,' he said mundanely, as the waiter poured. His words suggested the root of his interest; that she represented a challenge. 'Why is a beautiful, young Polish woman repairing antique compasses in a shop in London?'

Marianna had never been called beautiful before; at just twenty-five, she felt timelessly and exhaustedly old. She blushed, decided to hide behind the story of her grandfather.

'My grandparents, and the generations before them, as far back as I know, lived in Gdańsk.'

'Shipyards?' he asked, using all his knowledge.

'Yes. But it goes back much further. We have a long seafaring tradition. A nautical tradition.'

'Poland?'

She caught his eye quickly, looked away.

'It is not just the British who sail.'

'Of course.'

'My family were never seafaring, but they worked in the yards, builders and merchantmen.'

'You grew up in Gdańsk?'

He made the effort to try to pronounce the name the Polish way, the soft *n*, and she smiled. He recognised the beauty of her lips, the sadness in her eyes, obscured by her dark hair.

'Warsaw. But we visited Gdańsk every year. I loved the docks, the museum, the old shops.'

The duck arrived, hugging the center of the enormous plate, as if the outer edges had negotiated a deal to be food-free.

That night she went back to his apartment and had sex for the first time with someone other than her father.

4

'What have you been spending your money on now?'

The Gardener looked over the top of the Times.

'What are you talking about?'

He had forgotten about the small brass box. About to put on the washing, the Gardener's Wife fished the compass out of his trouser pocket, turned it over in her fingers. She opened it, read the note.

The words were on her lips, but she stopped herself. The Gardener had gone back to reading the paper. She slipped the note back inside and closed the lid.

Elyot was aware of wanting something he couldn't have, of desire sharpened by the impossible. How often is the ordinary, the acceptable and successful ordinary, cast aside in search of the thing that can't be had? Like so many, he longed for someone who was gone. Yet he liked the notion of a lost love, the impossibility of doomed romance, the eternal lovers who were never meant to be. It seemed suitably tragic for him, for he was a poet at heart, (if a poet who did not write.)

Every Friday he took the train to Paddington, the Bakerloo to Oxford Circus, then walked along Oxford Street to the junction of Tottenham Court Road and Charing Cross Road. At nine-thirty a.m., when he knew Marianna would be drinking coffee and slowly eating a pain au chocolat, never getting pastry on her lips, he would walk from teashop to coffee house, looking for her. An endless, romantic search.

He even found himself in a small, Polish delicatessen, describing the object of his desire and feeling foolish. The shopkeeper had smiled, had said that yes, he did have a customer – or two, or three – who met that description. Elyot formulated a plan to spend an entire week sitting in the café across the road, waiting for her to appear, although the plan did not happen.

Eventually he missed a Friday, and although he berated himself and made sure that the following week he was back on Charing Cross Road, it was not long before he missed another. As the months turned into a year, more Friday's than not, Elyot would not take the train.

He was not to know that every morning Marianna now took coffee at a small café around the corner from her apartment, before taking the train to work. The hours spent walking up and down Charing Cross Road were perfectly romantic, and perfectly destined to fail.

Once, every couple of months, Marianna would go back to their old café on the off-chance that Elyot would be there. One day they even missed each other by a little less than twenty minutes. But that was the type of relationship they had.

* * *

Marianna wore socks in bed, despite everything Burke said.

He told himself that the woman he had first encountered, huddled over a small compass in a small shop, had been sexy and vibrant and alive. In truth, he had found someone who would marry him, that was all. She had been the very essence of her employment; intricate, fascinating, intelligent, rewarding to greater study and interest; but there was only one person in London who thought Marianna alluring, and it wasn't Burke.

So Burke's memory changed to suit his needs, to create excuses. In this instance, it was the need he had to stay out late, to spend as little time with his wife and baby daughter as he could: to have other women.

He bought Marianna satin and lace nightwear so he could be annoyed when she never wore it. And when he crawled into bed, smelling of another woman's shower gel, and his feet touched hers, he would pull away and think dismal thoughts about how unattractive his wife was that she wore socks in bed.

* * *

Elyot was drinking coffee, his life conducted around it. Li Na was beseeching him. He felt dreadfully uncomfortable, his head low. His spoon tapped occasionally against the saucer.

'I don't understand,' said Li Na. 'You're a practical person, you live in the real world. There's no *one*. There's no magical *one*. There are over seven billion people out there. How can there be a *one*?'

Their relationship had dragged on longer than intended. A fun night had become a long weekend, then a month, then the next. *Trapped by eastern lovemaking* he joked to his colleagues, who couldn't understand why he didn't just leave. Finally he had forced the conversation.

'I didn't say that,' he said. He couldn't look up. The waitress watched the breakup from behind the counter.

'Well, what then?'

Li Na imagined she could change his mind. As if feelings could be manipulated, shaped by badgering and coercion.

Everyone says *I love you*. Everyone says *I'll always love you*. Words are tossed around like autumn leaves in the wind. Sometimes they are well meant. Sometimes the feeling lasts forever, sometimes the feeling dies. But what does anyone think when their partner is walking away? Those who plead? Those who write songs imploring their love not to go? What *are* they thinking? That you can recreate the passion, the ardour, and the love by guilt and desperation?

Elyot had never even told Li Na that he loved her. Nevertheless, his insides had curled into a tortured ball. He hated where he was, sitting in a small café, breaking up with the girl, seemingly the one at fault, his every word open to the closest inspection. Every single word.

He was about to crack, he was about to utter some meaningless phrase about giving it another go, when she stood up, stared down at him with one last, lingering look of loathing, and stormed from the café.

Relief embraced Elyot like a long lost love.

The waitress waited what she considered to be a decent interval before appearing at his table.

'Can I get you another coffee?' she smiled.

5

The Gardener's Wife allowed herself many bitter thoughts. A handwritten note placed inside an antique compass. The words themselves were not important. Even she could see the impossible romance of it. If only there had been a time and a place, she could have gone there and found her husband with the other woman. But there was nothing. Just five words, written in pencil.

She had a hundred confrontational conversations in her head with her husband, but none of them turned out well.

Several weeks later she threw the compass into the river near Battersea Power Station.

'Would you like another coffee?'

Elyot had just come on duty, his first day on the job, and was clearing up the few deserted tables. He had watched Marianna for a second, her head bowed over the foreign newspaper, earphones in.

When he spoke, she looked up, surprised. Her eyes were beautiful, welcoming him in from his reserve. Full of depth and sadness. He felt a peculiar moment of shock, but did not recognise in her curious expression that she felt the same, that she saw the same in his eyes.

She removed the earphones, but didn't answer.

'What are you listening to?' asked Elyot, surprising himself that the words were out there.

A moment, and then Marianna ran her hand across the screen of her phone so that it lit up. Dylan, *Self Portrait*.

'Wow,' said Elyot, smiling. 'I thought I was the only one who still listened to that.'

She smiled, but didn't have any words for him. Unused to conversation, and unsure what else to say, Elyot repeated, 'Another coffee?'

She shook her head, held his gaze for another enthralling few seconds, a moment that trapped them both in a silent world, and then she snapped from the trance, and looked back at the newspaper.

Elyot hesitated, wondering what to do with the moment, then

he took his tray and returned behind the counter, forgetting to lift her cup. The other waiter, Harrison, was waiting for him.

'She only ever has one cup. Same every day. Cup of coffee, pain au chocolat. Reads the newspaper. She's Polish.'

That night Elyot thought about Marianna, and she thought about him. Lying in bed, the city of London between them. Wondering what had been spoken in silence, and if they would see each other the following day.

Next morning, Elyot started early and was ready with her coffee and pain au chocolat. She seemed surprised, although he noticed that today she'd removed her earphones as soon as she'd entered the shop. She smiled, but never spoke. He said a few words, friendly, mundane words that he would come to repeat. They both saw the beauty in it, the unspoken attraction.

He thought he could say something more significant the following day, yet the following day never came. None of the conversations he had in his head ever crossed the threshold of his lips. All the things he wanted to say.

And so they developed a relationship of thought and unspoken intention, plus a few words from Elyot on the weather or the coffee or the pastries or *Knocked Out Loaded*. They could sense moods, they created histories, they imagined telepathy.

Some days Elyot accepted his inability to break free from small words; some days it depressed him, so that he took the depression home with him. Some nights he lay morosely in bed, unable to sleep. The next day his mood would be grim, she sensed the anger in him, didn't understand it. It was as if he was annoyed at her, and it reminded her of her mother.

Those days passed unhappily for them both. Eventually Elyot's mood would go, the smile and the enjoyment of the elusive romance would return. Marianna came and went with Elyot's moods, and tried to understand.

When the Owner started talking about giving the café a makeover, Elyot instantly objected. He didn't care what the café looked like, he didn't care how the business went, he no longer even needed to work there, having picked up some steady research work from a professor at the Greenwich Maritime Institute.

'You'll ruin the aesthetic,' said Elyot, desperately.

The Owner barked a laugh.

'So will closing the place down.'

'You don't need the money,' said Elyot, moderating his tone.

'You're this gentleman café proprietor. You do this for the love of it.'

'Very perceptive,' said the Owner. 'Aesthetics are fine, but so are customers.'

'We have customers,' said Elyot, with no conviction.

'For the love of God,' said the Owner.

Harrison glanced at Elyot; he knew which customer he was worried about. But Harrison would be leaving anyway. 'My friends,' the Owner went on, 'we are lost without connectivity.'

The Friday before the changes, Elyot was determined to talk to Marianna; but when the moment came, he deferred the conversation to the Monday. He talked about the pastries, while Marianna nodded behind beautiful eyes.

As she was leaving that day she turned and looked back at the counter. Elyot lifted his head from the coffee machine. They exchanged a look, which somehow seemed to have more significance than usual. As if their funny little romance was coming to an end. She smiled awkwardly, an embarrassed smile, and left the café.

They did not see each other again for twenty-one months and twenty-one days.

6

The compass did not sink. It was small and light, there was air trapped inside. It floated down river, slowly with the movement of the water. Dwarfed by the river and the city, an unnoticeable object drifting slowly away, past the Houses of Parliament, the London Eye, the landmarks of civilisation. Some days it washed up on the stones. Some days it got swept up in the wake of a ferry. Some days it bobbled against river walls. The compass was taking its time.

Once Li Na had gone, Elyot was able to relax about going to London. No longer needing to lie, he had more freedom, he had renewed passion, and he set himself the task of finding Marianna in a city of eight million. He felt he had fate on his side, as though there was an inevitability that the impossible romance would happen.

He took to going to London twice a week. He knew the time she took coffee in the morning, knew that she was a woman of habit. He made a directory of every café, every coffee shop, every tearoom in London. He would search them all if he had to.

In the catalogue of near misses that was their relationship, he quickly glanced into the coffee shop on the Kings Road that was her new home. But now she was drinking coffee half an hour earlier than previously, as she was taking breakfast before travelling to work. He had not included this in his calculations.

So when Elyot and Marianna found each other, at a small auction house in Bath, it was completely by accident and a moment for which neither of them had prepared. Suddenly, drifting through a market, searching for an old compass, they found themselves standing at the same table.

Elyot had lifted a Francis Barker & Son, manufactured in the late 19th century. Little more than an inch in diameter, blued steel needle, sunburst dial, brass case. There was a small sign saying *Do Not Touch*. Elyot removed the lid and was holding the compass much more delicately than was required.

He felt the presence beside him and turned quickly. She was standing four feet away, her eyes on his fingers. She had been looking at him, but lowered her gaze before he turned. He stared at her lips. Pale and soft, slightly parted. His breath caught in his throat. Slowly she raised her eyes.

It was somehow an impossible moment. She couldn't speak, was not even going to try. She felt the briefest, most glorious second of wonderful, blazing warmth. A moment of perfection, when nothing else mattered. A blissful instant in time.

Then slowly, something made him lower his gaze. He was not observant, he did not notice detail, not with anyone else he had ever known. But Marianna was different. And those long, slender fingers, the ones which he knew would be creative and technical, the ones which he had stared at and imagined running softly all over his body, now had a ring around the fourth finger; a ring with two large stones, stones which sparkled in the dim light of the hall.

She dropped her gaze to her fingers, their eyes stayed on the ring that Burke had bought the previous month. Elyot felt a peculiar sensation. Everything breaking down, melting away. All hope lost.

'You find what you're looking for?'

Marianna lowered her eyes farther at Burke's approach, feeling her face redden. Elyot quickly glanced at him. Every piece of clothing cried wealth, and Elyot instantly placed the compass back on the table and turned away.

He was lost in the crowd and Marianna did not even feel that she could watch him go. It was over. The moment she had dreamed about, the moment on which she had focused so much of her emotional energy for so long. There should have been a Big Bang, an instant in time from which so much could grow and develop. Instead, that moment was already disappearing into the crowd, walking out the door.

Burke noticed she was flushed but was not going to create any awkwardness by mentioning it. Everyone has ghosts, he thought, and he wasn't about to resurrect any of Marianna's.

He touched her arm, she shook her head to bring herself back to the present. She lifted the compass, so that her fingers were touching the same thing that Elyot's fingers had been touching a few seconds previously.

'Yes,' she said. 'This is... it is a Francis Barker. A nice piece.'

'Fantastic,' said Burke. 'Come on, let's go and get a drink before the whole thing kicks off.'

She placed the compass back on the table. She would get it now, it didn't matter the price. Even if someone else wanted it as much as she did, she would have Burke sitting beside her. Even though he might have sensed something of what had just transpired over this simple compass, he would do her bidding.

As they walked back through the crowd, she turned and looked at the compass on the table. In her mind it was already inexorably linked to Elyot, this small, circular brass box. At last she would have something that had been his, however briefly, and some infinitesimal part of her life was complete.

7

For a time the compass was lost. Lost from human knowledge, at least, if not lost in itself. How can a compass ever be lost?

Marianna and Burke never fought. In the place where they had gone, there was no need. They slept in the same bed; they shared in decisions regarding Ella; they ate dinner together on occasion, sometimes they went to the theatre. He didn't often take her to work events as he thought she might be awkward and clumsy socially. She had long ago given up wanting to be asked.

It had been three years and seven months since they'd made love; more than six years since they'd shared any intimacy of conversation. Marianna wasn't counting. But she could measure in days the only two things that were important to her. It was four years, three months and seventeen days since Ella had been born; five years, ten months and two days since the day that Burke had paid too much for the Francis Barker.

She presumed he'd forgotten which compass he'd bought for her that day, but Burke knew exactly which one it was, he knew that she was never going to sell it. He had seen the look on Elyot's face, Marianna's flush. One day he intended finding that compass and casually tossing it into a London bin. However, as with so many of his intentions regarding Marianna, it was something he never bothered doing, because he never really cared enough.

* * *

Elyot gave up for a while after the meeting at the auction house in Bath. He had seen the ring and the man, he thought he could not compete. Too close to the situation to recognise that Marianna had been overcome with the same shock of excitement and desire that he'd felt. It was only Burke, the detached one, who had noticed everything.

Elyot moved back to London, although he travelled often. Drowned in maritime research, freelance work, wherever it came. He gained a name for himself, work came easily.

Sometimes women seduced him, but Elyot was detached.

They recognised his melancholy, and it made him more attractive. But sex was always lonely and dispassionate, and every single woman that seduced him eventually acknowledged to herself that she had failed. Elyot was far out of reach.

Depression and frustration came and went, but as he grew older he became more accepting. He drank less alcohol, he spent his evenings like he spent his days, and gradually he became indispensable to those for whom he worked.

Eventually time allowed him to rekindle hope. He gave up on trying to find Marianna through coffee, and switched to antiques. He searched the directories, he searched online. The first time he visited her shop it was closed. He travelled around the country; Kings Lynn, Plymouth, as far north as Eyemouth. Small shops selling antique compasses. He would arrive with a little hope but no expectation; he might find something that would help with his work, but that would be an unlikely and unnecessary accident. The world of antique compasses was not big; if he had met Marianna once, it could happen again. He felt bound to her by it.

He walked past her shop regularly for three years; all the while she was at home with Ella. A shop that never opened, but which never closed down. A mystery that drew him in, and he wondered if Marianna could be at the heart of it. Every now and again he would see a sign that someone had been inside. He could see the mail had been lifted from behind the glass door. The few compasses in the window did not grow dusty.

One morning he slipped a note beneath the door. A few simple words that might send Marianna back to their old café. No time, no place, nothing that would bring a stranger to his table.

One day in four years Burke, unexpectedly in the vicinity, offered to lift the mail at the shop. An hour and a half after Elyot had left the note for Marianna, Burke lifted it and read it. Burke did not completely understand, he did not automatically connect the note to the man at the auction house in Bath. Yet he was no fool. The note was scrunched into his pocket, and later put in the bin

Gradually, Elyot's hopes for the shop faded, and he visited less and less, until he visited no more.

Wisława Szymborska
„miłość od pierwszego wejrzenia :)

8

Marianna returned to work when Ella was four and a half and started school. On the first day she went to the old café, looking for Elyot. Despite the fact that it no longer looked like the place where they had met, she liked the thought that he might be there. She took to going every day. She had the compass in her pocket, and the sense of him in a place they had once known.

A few months later she had not tired of the idea; she enjoyed the café, despite the fact that it might as well have been a Starbucks or Café Nero. She sat at the same table, when it was free, she listened to the same old Dylan albums, she imagined Elyot still there, serving coffee. And all the time her melancholy grew.

Eventually, she decided to set the compass free, to let it go, to let the compass find him. She knew the notion was absurd, yet she trusted in it. The compass had brought them together once before, and it would do so again.

She wrote a few words on a small piece of paper, placed it inside the compass, and left the compass sitting on a park bench. The next day she sat in the café at the usual time and waited for Elyot to arrive.

That evening she received a call from Poland. Her mother had died. The next day, walking away from her marriage, and Elyot, and the compass, and her impossible romance, she took Ella to Poland to visit her homeland. They stayed for six months.

* * *

When Marianna and Ella returned to London, Burke had given up on them and had moved his things from the house. Marianna did not weep, Ella barely noticed. The next day Ella went back to school, Marianna went to Burke's office.

She felt strangely uplifted, and did not understand why. She had thought herself so disinterested in Burke she would not even have been pleased by his leaving.

'Are we getting a divorce?' she asked.

'I don't know yet,' said Burke. 'I lost you so long ago, it doesn't seem to matter whether we're still married.'

They had never spoken of it, but she understood. She had been lost to him, as sure as if she had disappeared one day at the shop, never to return. The marriage had been her mistake.

As she left his office she put her hand in her pocket to touch the compass, something she still did several times a day; but it was gone, because six months earlier she had left it sitting on a park bench.

* * *

Elyot had his feet propped on a desk, eating a maple and pecan Danish. The night before he'd had dinner with a fellow researcher. Same age, same interests, it had been very easy. Sex had been more or less inevitable. She had left his apartment at thirty-six minutes after midnight. He was currently sitting in as relaxed a pose as possible to try to look cool when she came in. He'd never slept with a colleague before, and wasn't sure how he should be arranged at his desk.

He had come in early so he would already be in position, looking nonchalant, when she arrived. He felt vaguely ridiculous, yet wondered if she would want to see him again that evening. He would be worried if she did, and slightly offended if she didn't.

At 8:37 that morning, as he placed the last of the maple and pecan in his mouth, the compass found its way back to him.

'Did you see this?' said Larkin, placing the compass in front of Elyot. 'How'd it go last night, by the way?' he added, walking over to his own desk, flipping the Guardian to the sports section.

Elyot stared at the compass. Little more than an inch across, brass case, slightly discolored by drifting on the river and lying on the banks for a few months, before floating up on the shore by the Royal Naval College at Greenwich.

'Where?' was all he managed to say.

'Jorkiss, you know, the security guy. Said it was in the river, right up against the bank. Just out there. Might be quite old, take a look.'

Elyot's fingers were already resting on it. A compass in a small brass box. It could have been any compass in the world, but he knew which one it was. He eased the lid off with his thumbnail, a small piece of paper fell onto the desk.

He glanced over his shoulder. Jane was walking in, trying not to look at him. A minute earlier he would have been overanalyzing her awkward glances. Now he looked right through her. He turned back to the compass, took in the simple beauty of the needle and the sunburst dial, then he opened the small piece of paper.

Five words. That was all.

He stared at it for a few moments then looked quickly up at the clock. There was still time. Maybe it was months too late, or years too late, but he knew it wouldn't be. He stood quickly, lifting the compass.

'I'll be back later,' he said, and without waiting ran quickly from the office.

Jane watched him go, curious as to why she'd had that much of an effect on him.

'God, what'd you do to him last night?' said Larkin, smiling.

* * *

Marianna turned at the movement of the door. She wouldn't usually look around; she wasn't an observer of life. She never watched people. She was stuck in her own world, where the constants were.

Elyot hesitated at the doorway, until someone muttered at him to stop letting in the draught. He took a step into the café, and then quickly came and sat down across from her at the table. She had been about to leave, hating herself for the six months in Poland, signing forms, clearing up her mother's affairs.

She removed her earphones, but didn't turn off the music. *Desire* buzzed tinnily between them. This time, strangely, there was no elation, no blinding flash. They were sitting across a table from one another, the compass had chosen the moment, and they would be together. For a second they held each other's gaze, and then they looked down at the small compass that Elyot had placed on the table.

No one noticed them.

'I got your note,' said Elyot, simply.

Marianna smiled. He couldn't remember seeing her smile like that before. The smile of his memory had been circumspect.

'Would you like that coffee?'

'Thank you,' she said. 'That would be lovely.'

Unable to take his eyes from her, he slowly got to his feet.

'Have you been looking for me?' she asked.

'Yes.'

She smiled, her fingers rested on the lid of the compass.
'We're here now,' he added.
'Yes,' said Marianna.
And from then on, words engulfed them.

The Elephant At The Table

Erin had planned it for a few weeks, but when she finally brought the third cup of coffee to the breakfast table, and made the joke, she got the line wrong.

'This is for the elephant in the room,' she meant to say. Instead, it came out as, 'This is for the elephant at the table,' which allowed Jon to laugh at her. It wasn't as though he didn't know what she meant, and later she Googled it, and plenty of people said 'the elephant at the table' in any case.

But that was how the elephant was first mentioned, and that was how Jon managed to pivot away from why the elephant was actually there.

'Nothing for the elephant?' he said at breakfast the next morning with a smile. This time, at least, the smile vanished when he saw the look on her face.

* * *

Some day, Erin knew, they would have to have the conversation. They'd been living together for three years, and after the initial romance there had followed the sad, slow decline.

That day she had lunch at the small café just off Leicester Square where she and Molly met every Tuesday.

'Did you do the elephant line yet?' asked Molly.

Erin nodded, then shook her head, indicating it hadn't worked.

'Wait,' said Molly, 'seriously? You said there's this huge thing we're not talking about, we can't ignore it, and you still didn't talk about it?'

'The news was on,' said Erin, weakly.

Molly rolled her eyes, not at all surprised.

'You don't think he's having an affair?'

'It's not that,' said Erin. 'We don't want to be together anymore, but neither of us knows how to start the conversation.'

'You're going to have to come out with it!'

'I can't.'

'Maybe you could prepare the spare room for the elephant,' said Molly, 'that might get Jon's attention.'

'Maybe if I had an affair with the elephant,' said Erin, and they laughed.

* * *

That evening at dinner, Erin set the table for three. She stopped short of making a third plate of spaghetti, but she did pour a glass of wine for the new addition to their relationship.

When Jon came downstairs he stopped, then quickly realised what she'd done, and smiled. Over dinner he talked about his day at work. He did get Erin to talk about the theatre project she was working on, the one with the Irish playwright everyone was excited about, although she thought his questions automatic, stilted, going through the motions, and soon enough he brought the subject back to himself.

When she was clearing up, Erin didn't bother removing the third setting.

That night, lying in bed, she thought about that place setting, deciding it really oughtn't to be for an elephant, but for the next man in her life.

Yes, she had her work, and she didn't want to be defined as the kind of woman who needed a man to justify her existence, but it would be so nice to have someone to whom she could talk, that was all.

* * *

The idea of the third place setting was quickly absorbed into their lives, and was no longer commented upon. Similarly, the idea they were sharing their relationship with another man, one with whom Erin could have long, meaningful conversations, soon became part of Erin's fantasy life. The other man was there when she needed him, long conversations in her head, a make-believe romance she could take to bed.

* * *

One day Jon came into the kitchen unexpectedly, catching her talking out loud. Erin had an awkward moment, wondered how much he'd heard her say, and then, typically, Jon acted as though it hadn't happened. He poured them both a glass of wine, and asked how long it was until dinner.

That evening Erin knew things were a little different. It seemed at last that Jon was ready. Getting caught talking to herself had been embarrassing, but perhaps it was the catalyst they'd needed.

Eating in silence, that Norah Jones CD playing softly, she could see Jon turning the words over in his head. If they stalled on his lips, would she herself be able to force them out?

'There's something I've been meaning to say,' said Jon, his voice quietly finding its way out into the world.

Thank goodness, thought Erin. The word *freedom* appeared in her head.

'Sorry I've seemed distant recently,' said Jon, 'just had a lot on my mind at work.'

He hesitated, and she wondered for a moment if he was finished, then he nodded to himself as he reached into his pocket.

The shock of what was about to happen hit Erin like a thunderbolt, as Jon lifted his hand and placed a small box on the table.

A black, leatherette ring box.

He held her gaze, swallowing loudly.

'Erin... ' he began.

'I'm leaving!' she blurted out.

The words remained in the air for a while, bouncing off the walls, colliding with the couple as they sat at the table briefly suspended in hopeless impotence.

'What?' said Jon, finally.

'I'm sorry,' said Erin. 'This thing... I can't do it anymore.'

They held each other's gaze for a few more moments, but at last the words had been spoken. Erin instinctively took another mouthful of food, but it was like eating dirt.

She dabbed at her lips with a napkin, then pushed her chair away.

'I'm sorry, Jon,' she said, and this time she couldn't even look at him. And then she was up and out the room.

Jon watched her go, looking at the space where he'd last seen her, as though she had left something of herself behind, and then he turned sadly to the empty place setting.

He moved the small box towards it, and opened it. The box was empty.

'Sometimes you just have to force these things,' said Jon to the elephant, his voice heavy with regret. 'And now we know.'

The elephant had nothing to say. The elephant, in fact, was no longer there. Jon lifted his fork and took another mouthful of food.

Touch Of The Spider

(A DI Westphall Story)

The cyclist has been dead for over an hour. Claire Stuyvesant, hit from behind by a car, rear wheel buckled, bike tossed off to the side, body punted twenty yards down the road. Her neck is unnaturally bent, making it impossible to look at her without wincing. Eyes open, staring at the sky, head twisted, lying on her front.

There's a cold wind coming up the glen. A single-track road, now blocked in either direction. With it being a cul-de-sac, there are never many cars up this way in any case. Emily Borden, the victim's neighbour, living at the top of the glen, got out of her car, and stood staring at the body for a while. She seemed curious, a little concerned, rather than shocked. After we took a preliminary statement and arranged for someone to visit her again later today, she drove her Land Rover Discovery over the heather at a thirty degree angle, around the scene of the crime.

Dr Sanderson, the pathologist out from Inverness, approaches, removing thin latex gloves as he comes.

'Detective Inspector Westphall,' he says, 'nice to see you getting your hands dirty.'

'Doctor,' I nod, in return.

Detectives wouldn't usually attend a road traffic accident, but the police on the scene called it in straight away, this being the third cyclist killed within a week.

'Brutal death,' says Sanderson. 'Thrown forward, obviously, tried to break her fall with her right arm. Snapped like a twig.'

He pauses for a moment, and I can sense him rejecting the cliché, wishing he'd thought of something more original. 'Neck buckled on impact. I'd say there's one clean break in her arm, but her neck is a mess. You know how many vertebrae there are in the neck?'

I probably should.

'Seven,' he says, when I don't answer. 'They've all been crushed.'

He glances back at the corpse, then looks over the scene. One ambulance, two paramedics, three police cars, seven officers. Hills on either side, the flat grey of a dull early autumn day lifted by the luminescent purple of the heather. No moisture in the cold air. Up the glen, keeping a watchful eye, a herd of deer. In the field beside us, sheep, standing as far away from the action as possible.

‘Lovely spot for it,’ says Sanderson after a while.

I can feel the dead cyclist weep for the husband she’ll never hold again. Her spirit lingers, unable, or unwilling to break free. She is the hair standing on the back of my neck, the shiver that touches my spine. I know that she will not remain with the corpse. She will be my companion.

* * *

Standing with Detective Sergeant Sutherland in the ops room back at the station, looking at the photographs of the three victims. One woman, two men. They’d all been wearing Lycra, in the bright colours of the day. The first victim – Tom Culrose – took a direct hit from the front. Abdomen flattened, then, in the estimation of the SOCOs, the driver had reversed over the body, one of the tyres slipping off the skull onto the neck. The other two – Stuyvesant and Dan McGowan – were struck from behind. Similar effect, though McGowan’s back was broken. Unlike the others, he was still technically alive when he was discovered. Died in the ambulance on the way to Inverness.

‘If we narrow the potential perpetrators down to every motorist in the UK who hates cyclists,’ says Sutherland, ‘we can reduce the list of suspects to fifteen million.’

Lovely dry delivery. Sutherland takes a bite of doughnut, chews for a moment, then has a slug of coffee.

Three separate incidents, in three different locations, more than fifty miles apart. No link between the victims. Culrose, a mechanic, 51; Stuyvesant, an architect, 33; McGowan, retired fisherman from Wick, 60.

‘I don’t buy it,’ I say.

Sutherland takes another glug from the cup, then uses it to indicate the board.

‘What?’ he asks, simply.

‘I know you were joking about every driver hating these guys, but that’s still the go-to explanation. We’re all thinking it. The only thing that connects them is fluorescent Lycra. Our killer had just had enough, but they didn’t see red, they saw luminous lime green.

‘That’s what I’m not buying.’

Sutherland tips the rest of the cup of coffee into his mouth, and then uses the empty cup to point at the board again.

‘What d’you think?’

I can feel the sadness of Claire Stuyvesant. She's here with us, as much as the whiteboard, and the table, and the seven chairs, and the ficus benjamina that gives life to this cold, windowless room where the bodies of investigations are dissected.

'Someone wanted one of these people dead, and so they killed the others to make it look like a thing. That's what we need to do. Pin down that one, and then we'll find the others were random. So, for the moment, three separate murder enquiries, working on the basis that two of them will go nowhere. Who wanted one of these people dead? That's the question.'

Sutherland takes a drink from the empty cup. 'Not bad,' he says.

* * *

Neighbours see things. They know. Of less use to the investigating officer if they're friends with the victim or they fought over the height of the garden hedge. However, if they're disinterested, they will still have seen who came and went, they will still have heard words spoken too loudly.

* * *

'Always putting things in bins,' says Dan McGowan's neighbour.

An old row of terraced houses in Lairg. Fascinating little woman, bent double, a walking stick, round spectacles, hair in a net.

'What d'you think he put in the bins?'

There's a pause. We can hear her sucking teeth.

'Body parts.'

She sniggers.

* * *

'Lovely music,' says Emily Borden, who'd seemed detached to find her neighbour, Claire Stuyvesant, dead in the middle of the road. 'That's what I'll remember. Didn't see the husband much. Travels a lot. Something in banking. Works in Edinburgh, far as I know.' He works in Inverness. 'We didn't really talk much.'

'What kind of music?'

'Classical. Such a broad term. All sorts. Big, sweeping orchestral pieces a lot of the time, now that I think about it. Choral too. And string quartets.'

'While she worked?'

'Yes. It's a nice studio, with a view down the glen. She'd have the window open in spring and summer. Autumn, if it wasn't too cold.'

A pause, a wistful look in the direction of the glen, even though we can't see it from where we're sitting.

'She liked Walton. Guess they'll have *Nimrod* at the funeral. What d'you think?'

'*Nimrod* was Elgar.'

'Oh.'

* * *

'Had it coming.'

Some neighbours are angry. Tom Culrose's neighbour is angry.

'Go on.'

'Every damn evening,' he says. 'I mean, don't get me wrong, we got on fine, Tom and I. At least, we never spoke to each other, which is all you can ask of a neighbour, right?'

It's what Jesus would have said.

'Go on,' I say again.

'Brought his work home with him, didn't he? Every evening, had a car out there, jacked up, clanking away with a doofer.'

'A doofer?'

'A thing. I don't know what it's called. But, I mean, you can't repair a car without making a lot of noise, can you? Just not possible. And it's not just me, everyone along this street was fed up with it. Ask them.'

We already have. He's not wrong.

'Did you all complain?'

'Of course. Told us to bugger off, didn't he?'

'Did you complain to the local police?'

'Huh,' he says, with accompanying eye roll. 'Same answer.'

'You think someone might've been annoyed enough to take matters into their own hands?'

He leans forward, a snarl on his lips. Holds the stare. We've asked the question of six people along this street so far, and every one of them has given the same answer.

'I don't know who out of this lot would've had the *cojones*,' he says, 'but I'd've given them an alibi if they'd asked.'

* * *

When I go to bed, Claire Stuyvesant is still with me. I have become her passage from this world. She cannot let go while there is unfinished business.

I sense dead people around me. I have not looked for it. I do not look for them. There is nothing logical in this irrational notion. They come, or not. Sometimes they talk. Sometimes they hover on the edge of consciousness, a feeling, rather than a physical presence.

How can I ever read anything in to it? Are they there at all, or is it just me, my subconscious, creating an ephemeral vision? Plucking something from the air around me that does not exist?

I lie in bed, one hand behind my head, the other resting on my stomach. I don't know where Claire Stuyvesant is. Standing next to me? Lying in the bed? Sitting on the floor in a corner, knees drawn up, head hung low, weeping? I cannot tell. Yet I know she is here, and neither Dan McGowan nor Tom Culrose are present. If they have stopped off somewhere before departing this world, it is not with me.

So what brings Claire Stuyvesant to my bedroom, late at night, on the day of her murder?

It is more personal with her. Why else is she here? The first two were the cover. Claire Stuyvesant, the third kill, was the intended victim all along. It may well be that the cover story is not complete, and there will be more death before this is done.

* * *

'And your wife got on well with the neighbours? There aren't many of you up at the far end of the glen.'

Interview at the station with Alan Stuyvesant, the widow. Flew in last night from a business trip to Berlin. Tired and red-eyed, possibly self-medicated. Long stares off into nowhere.

He looks up, shakes his head, tries to draw himself back to the present, picks the question out of the past.

'You know… she was great. Claire was great, she really was. Got along with everyone.'

I give him a moment, waiting to see if there's a follow-up, but I can see his eyes drift away. I glance at Sutherland, who shrugs in response.

'How about Mrs Borden?' I ask.

There's no actual reason why I should be asking that question, other than a hunch. I can't take a hunch into court.

He drags himself back from the great beyond, focuses on me, takes a moment to recall the question, then says, 'Mrs Borden?'

We stare at each other while he thinks about it. Some seconds pass. I don't rush him. Time is elastic.

I read something in his eyes. Another hunch.

'It's fine, Mr Stuyvesant,' I say, 'we won't keep you. I know how difficult it must be for you at the moment. We'll see you out. Go home, take care of whatever it is you need to, and we'll speak to you again tomorrow morning.'

Heavy sigh, drawn from the depths. Eyes on the table he rises. Sutherland and I rise with him.

Shake my head, noticing the cobweb above the door.

'Goddam spiders,' I say. 'Every damn autumn.'

Sutherland and Stuyvesant glance up. No one is terribly interested. Idle words tossed out and left behind, as we leave the small room we use for witness interviews.

Alan Stuyvesant has no more words.

* * *

Sutherland and I stand by the window in the open-plan office, looking out on another grey morning, the crows in the autumn trees on Knockfarrel hill. Cup of coffee each, Sutherland clutching his regulation sugar-frosted.

'The cobweb line was a little transparent,' he says.

'You think he saw through it?'

'About the time he looked right into the CCTV camera.'

'Had to be sure we got a good image. Get it over to Borders and Customs, let's see if he really has been out the country for all of the last three weeks.'

* * *

If Alan Stuyvesant knows what's coming, he doesn't show it. He does not run, he does not react. Soon enough we have proof of him leaving Scotland two weeks ago, returning the next day on a false passport. Making the reverse trip after the death of his wife.

Using facial recognition software, we get him in Inverness, buying an old Range Rover, which he did using the same name as the passport. We haven't yet located the car, but we have footage of it in the vicinity of the murders. He was clever enough to avoid having any witnesses to the deaths, and he has Alfonse McIntyre, MA(Hons), Dip RCR, LLB, Dip LP, NP, the lawyer all these people want. But we have motive, and money, and false names, and enough to take to the procurator.

He sits in silence. He doesn't just refuse to answer questions, he doesn't speak at all.

'The middle-aged Lycra brigade can ride in peace,' says Sutherland caustically, as we leave the interview room.

* * *

The following afternoon, called to a hit and run on the 832 between Rosemarkie and Cromarty. A bike buckled and broken at the side of the road, a man in pink punted fifteen feet over a low fence into a field of sheep. The sheep fled.

Sutherland and I, in our familiar positions, surrounded by the usual array of emergency road accident staff. This time the road has a lane in either direction, and so we've been able to keep it open. Cars pass occasionally, they slow, they glance over. Sometimes someone will stop and ask, and we usher them on with a familiar platitude. We pay attention to every car that passes, because the killer who returns to the scene as soon, and as innocently, as possible, is not a rare beast.

'He must have an accomplice,' he says. 'It's obvious.'

'I don't know,' I say, nodding, acknowledging Sutherland's attempt to find us an out. A reason why we're right to have Alan Stuyvesant in custody, when the killer has struck again. To have made the arrest, to be preparing the charges. 'That silence of his. Maybe he was doing something completely unrelated that he doesn't want to own up to.'

'Like what?' says Sutherland, sceptical.

'We know very little about this man, Sergeant. People do things, people have things in their life. There is no way to tell until we have more information. Maybe he was having an affair…'

'That involved buying a beat-up old Range Rover?'

I don't have an answer, so let the question go.

'There are options here,' says Sutherland, 'but either way, he wasn't not involved. There's an accomplice in play, or else this has been done by someone entirely different, who just thought, the hell with it, open season on the MAMILs. Maybe it was an accident, the driver panicked, and thought, wait, I can just leg it and the police'll think it was the same killer as before. Whatever, Stuyvesant remains implicated in the first three deaths.'

'We need to get him to talk,' I say.

I agree with Sutherland, yet I have the nagging doubt that we've got it wrong. If we've got the right man, why is it that I can yet feel the haunting of Claire Stuyvesant? Her hand on my shoulder, her face leaning against my neck, her warm tears on my skin. I shiver, and reach unthinkingly into my pocket for my phone.

It rings.

'Alice?' I say, answering, turning away from Sutherland.

'Sir, I've found something,' says Constable Cole. 'You should get back here.'

I catch Sutherland's eye, click the phone off and slip it into my pocket.

* * *

We find Emily Borden at home, polishing the Discovery. The façade gleams in the pale afternoon sun, having just been washed, and when we arrive at her house, she is on her haunches, vigorously cleaning the bumper.

After a quick look over her shoulder at the sound of our arrival, she returns to her work.

We stand and watch her for a moment. If there was any surface evidence to be scrubbed from the bumper, it will already be gone. The chances that she will have accessed the on-board computer and scrubbed the analytics revealing the deactivation of the airbags, or the impact at the front of the car, are minimal. The bumper will also give up its clues, no matter how hard she wipes it down.

'You're under arrest,' says Sutherland.

Proved right, I'm happy to let him control the narrative of this short scene.

She stops rubbing, takes a moment, looks at the bumper, decides presumably that there's nothing else to be done, then glances over her shoulder.

'I don't think so,' she says. 'It's not a crime to clean your car in Scotland, is it?'

* * *

They sit silently together. We decided to place them side-by-side, handcuffed to the desk, watching the CCTV footage of them leaving the Highland Hotel in Wick, four weeks previously. Smiling as they went, another camera catching their kiss in the car, before they headed back out onto the A9.

'Doesn't prove a thing,' says Borden, when the short film is finished.

'Nope,' I say. Sutherland is behind, standing at the door, arms folded. Cole is on the other side of the small room, hands behind her back. 'I guess not. But we have enough to charge you, and we'll spend the next few weeks interviewing you, and this is the last time you'll see each other until you're taken into court, and when you're on your own, you'll break.'

'No, we won't,' she says, squeezing the words from between thin, bitter lips.

Stuyvesant tries to reach out to her, but the chains are marginally, and cruelly, just too short.

'Sergeant, take Mrs Borden back to her cell, please.'

She curses, loudly, dramatically, a single word spat in my direction. A drop of saliva lands on Stuyvesant's face, but he is impassive.

Sutherland roughly grabs her wrists, unlocks the handcuffs, drags her to her feet and marches her out of the room.

The door closes.

I'm not in the mood for game playing, hedging, talking around the subject, hoping we get a minor breakthrough.

'We do speak to other people, Mr Stuyvesant. We know about you and Claire fighting. We know about the shouting, and the slamming doors, Claire crying in the picture window, the lonely world of a remote Scottish glen for company. And we know that you and Emily Borden were having an affair. And you can fight it all the way if you want, but you know Mrs Borden. You know what type of person she is. We all know the Mrs Bordens of the world. She will not go lightly, and when it comes to it, she will throw everything under the bus as she tries to stay out of prison.'

A moment. He holds my gaze, then slowly his eyes slip away.

'That includes you,' I say.

Alan Stuyvesant swallows. He looks at Constable Cole. He does not have the conviction of a triple murderer, but culpability cloaks him like dust.

* * *

End of the day, Sutherland and I standing at the window of the office open-plan.

I no longer feel the presence of Claire Stuyvesant, and am no more surprised by this than I am by the unmasking of the murderous widow.

I was shadowed by the spirit for a reason, and now the reason is gone. Do spirits have any free will, or are they naturally occurring phenomena? They happen or they don't, they linger or not. The weight has been loosened, her killers have been unmasked, and the wraith has vanished. And now, the body in the mortuary aside, there is nothing of Claire Stuyvesant left on earth.

'Alice said he caved like a school kid,' says Sutherland, after taking a drink of tea.

'Yes,' I say, nodding. 'He did. You know the guilt is at its strongest when they don't even wait for the lawyer.'

'Mrs Borden on the other hand,' he says, making a small gesture with his cup. 'Might be time to open an investigation into that car accident that killed her husband four years ago.'

'Already got Alice looking at it,' I say.

There is a window open, the smell of an autumnal, smoky fire drifting in. We can hear the traffic heading out on the Strathpeffer road, the crows marking angry circles in the sky.

The Ringmaster

No one ever knew his real name. They called him the Ringmaster. And now he was dead, his body crushed and battered and broken in an attack that was bestial in its ferocity. His killer, in a final act of diabolical brutality, had slit open his stomach, sucked up his innards and then sprayed them around in a bloody fifty yard radius. The lungs, somehow containing the last vestiges of air, bounced into a far corner. The heart rolled over beside them, leaving a trail of aortic slime in its wake. It was nasty, but it was the Glasgow way.

When the deed was done, years of humiliation having been avenged, his killer returned to her small caravan, where her clothes and all her possessions were neatly laid out on the bed, ready to go. And so it was that at 4.37 on a June morning that had already dawned warm and bright, Nelly the Elephant packed her trunk and said goodbye to the circus.

Flying Birds

1

Stipe

A November dawn. Just before eight a.m. Stipe closed the door, automatically felt his pocket to make sure he had the key – something he invariably did, like now, the wrong way round – then looked up at the sky. A grey dawn, light cloud, clearer patches out over the Moray Firth. He could see neither the firth nor the estuary from his house, his view extending no further than the houses across the road, so if he wanted to watch the morning come in on the land, if he wanted to watch the early flight of the geese, he had to do what he was doing this morning. Get up, get out, walk through the town, down to the bay.

Two small piers, just below the Crown & Anchor.

On one, a dog walker, the border terrier on a lead, nosing around at the grass growing through the stones, taking a pee on the bollard. Another woman standing at the far edge, hands in pockets, a Vera hat pulled low over her head. She looked cold.

On the other, eight people in a ruptured line, each with a camera on a tripod. Stipe stood for a moment considering the two piers, and then walked to the one on the right where there was a man with a dog and a woman with a hat.

Out onto the short pier. The dog and its walker were approaching him, and he looked at the dog, prepared to engage. The dog wasn't interested, didn't notice him. The woman in the hat was looking out over the bay. Stipe approached, positioned himself far enough away from her that it would be clear he wasn't interested in conversation, and followed her gaze out over the water.

Thousands of geese. The wildlife people always put a number on it – fifteen thousand, twenty thousand, forty thousand – but to the layman with no idea how they arrived at that number, it was just a lot of geese. A bay-full.

Stipe didn't know anything about them. The where they came from, and where they were going of it. He wasn't interested in the process, just the spectacle. Same as pretty much everything else in which he took an interest. He didn't want to know how a photographer was able to take a great shot, what a writer was thinking, how many times a singer had to record a track. He didn't want to see the director's cut, or the ten minutes with the cameramen at the end of a nature documentary. He wasn't interested in the lives of the stars, he didn't want to know who had split up with whom, and what artistic enterprise had resulted. He wasn't interested in why mountain ranges had formed, or at what rate the continents were drifting apart. He wasn't interested in the science behind wind and tides, but he could stand and look at waves crashing on rocks for hours.

And so it was with the geese.

The noise of a sky full of geese was fantastic. The water was blanketed in them, the air was full of them, as they'd already started the morning flight out onto the Moray firth. Steam rose from the cacophony, the air was crisp and cold. Stipe pulled his coat close around him.

He noticed the small pile of clothes on the bollard next to the woman wearing the hat, and then he saw the movement in the water, the bald, middle-aged head bobbing towards the pier.

Swimming in early November. He was about to emerge from the cold water, shivering and blue, or red-skinned and bombastic. Either way, Stipe didn't want to be this close to them. He glanced over at the other pier, noted that none of the photographers were speaking to each other, and decided he would watch the geese from there.

As the bald man arrived at the pier and gave a grotesque splutter, clearing seawater from inside his head, Stipe turned away and walked quickly back along the short pier.

2

Ellen

All the lousy clichés… Lipstick on the collar, working late at the office, the aroma of a different soap, the unexplained ping of the phone, the weekend away… There had been none of it.

So, yes, David, it is *out of the blue*, she wanted to say. But there were no words. Nothing would form. There were no cohesive thoughts to put into words, and even if there had been, she found herself incapable of speaking.

'So, I don't know what to do.'

He looked at her, a helplessness about him, as though waiting for a suggestion. Looking to her to sort it out. She was the fixer, after all. She was the one who phoned the plumber, she was the one who arranged the house insurance, she was the one who put the car in for its MOT, she was the one who made sure the kids at university had enough money to buy food until the end of term. Logical then, that she should help her husband out with his tricky problem of him having fallen in love with Jan. *Jan in make-up, not Jan in sound.* Just for clarification.

Or perhaps it was not a solution he sought, but absolution. *On you go, I don't mind, I've been looking for you to leave anyway. Go to Jan in make-up. See how it goes. I'll wait for you, just in case you decide to come back, and I won't mind you stinking of remorse and millennialism and twenty-nine year-old pussy…*

Well, there was a cohesive thought.

She did not let the bitterness come to her face, she did not let the words cross her lips. She lowered her eyes, she could not look at him.

'I mean, look…'

Oh, fuck off…

Cohesive thoughts coming thick and fast all of a sudden.

'I'm not saying I'm in love with her, or anything. Obviously I still love you. I still… we still have this thing, right? You and I? We have our thing?'

She lifted her eyes. Five minutes previously she would have said they'd still had a thing. Whatever that thing had been, however, he'd just swiped it away with a slap of the hand, a snap of the fingers, a fifteen tonne nuclear weapon detonated beneath them.

There went the thing. There was no thing. Sounded like there hadn't been a thing in quite some time.

She didn't comment on the thing.

What could one say at this exact point in a relationship that hadn't been said a thousand, a million, times before? How many women had sat at a kitchen table as their husband broke the news? Why would she do any better than any of the previous scriptwriters?

They were now staring at the same spot on the table. Perhaps he took some solace in that small, shared moment.

He looked like he needed solace. If she wouldn't speak to him, if she wouldn't let him explain, if she wouldn't even talk to him, wasn't he the victim?

That, at least, appeared to be the thought process playing out across his face.

'I mean, look,' he began again, 'I don't know if it'll go anywhere, I really don't. All I'm asking is six months. I'll give it six months. And I know you might not want me back after that, but, I mean, we'll see, right? I don't want to just say, that's it. The thing with Jan, it's… I mean, who knows? Maybe once the lust plays out, there'll be nothing le…'

She cracked. Hand across the face, hard, fast, closed fist, caught him on the cheek with her engagement ring.

'Jesus!' he exclaimed, hand to his bloody cheek, the shock on his face. 'You *hit* me?'

'Oh, for fuck's sake,' she said, finally finding some words.

3

Stipe

Stipe looking out over the bay as he walked along the pier. The photographers had come well prepared, blessing this pier with the aroma of coffee. He'd thought about making some before he came out, bringing with him the orange thermos mug with the McLaren F1 logo on the side. Had decided instead to come empty-handed, allowing him to thrust his hands into his pockets.

He glanced at them as he walked past, unconsciously judging as he went. He had no idea who these people were, but he'd wager they'd arrived together on a minibus (he hadn't noticed a minibus), they were all bird watching geeks rather than photographers on the hunt for a good picture, and they could probably all bore anyone to death with several hours of excited goose-related chatter.

Three men, the wrong end of middle-aged, possible already retired; two women in their fifties; two younger men, side by side, possibly still in their teens; a young woman.

His eyes lingered a little longer on the young woman, then he forced himself to stare straight ahead again, and then he was at the end of the pier.

Above, the sky was a sea of geese. To the right, the tide continued to flood in through the narrow channel that led from the firth. Culbin forest was dark in early morning shadow on the other side of the bay.

He watched the birds, and while he did not wonder where they had come from or where they were going, he did at least wonder what effect the changing climate was having on them. Were there fewer birds than usual? If there were more, was it for some strange, counterintuitive, negative reason?

He may have asked himself the question, but he had no intention of asking any of the bird watchers. Maybe he'd look it up when he got home.

'It's amazing, right?'

Stipe glanced to his left. The young woman was now standing away from her camera, head lifted to the spectacle of the geese. A maroon beanie pulled down over her forehead, long, dark hair over her shoulders, an old-fashioned duffel coat. She was holding a beaker of coffee, no lid, steam rising into the air.

She was beautiful. That was why she had distracted him before.

'Yep,' was all he could think to say.

She didn't look at him, allowing him to look at her a little longer. Yes, beautiful.

'You're not taking any more photographs?' he asked.

'Nah,' she said. 'How many pictures of a billion geese in flight do you actually need? Thought I should look at them, rather than just take pictures. Got more than enough already with which to bore everyone to death on Instagram.'

She glanced at him, smiled, went back to looking at the birds.

Stipe look round at the rest of the bird watching crew. Most of the others did not share her desire to look naturally upon the flight of the geese, and remained trapped behind their equipment. Only one of the older women had detached herself, standing a few yards behind Stipe and the girl, hands in her pockets.

'You want a coffee?'

A beat. A snap of the fingers. A question from nowhere. He heard the tone, missed the words.

'Sorry?' he said.

He turned back to the girl. She was smiling again.

'You all right?' she said. 'You seem kind of distracted.'

She looked at the woman with her hands in her pockets, then at Stipe.

'Yeah, just zoned out for a moment. It happens.'

'A regular Walter Mitty, huh?'

'Yeah, Walter Mitty.'

One of those cultural references that had been there all his life. He'd never read the story, he'd never seen the Danny Kaye movie, he'd never seen the Ben Stiller movie, though he had, on innumerable occasions, had someone snap their fingers in front of his face and say, *hey, Walter Mitty!*

'You want a coffee?' she asked again.

'Sure,' said Stipe.

'Awesome. I always make too much. And most of these geeks aren't coffee drinkers. They're all so old. They drink tea, topped up with whisky.' She looked conspiratorially along the line, then lowered her voice and said, 'Even the two teenagers are like a hundred and fifty or something.'

She bent to her bag, took out another mug, poured the coffee from a large green flask, and handed the mug to Stipe.

'Lots of milk, no sugar, that OK?'

'Perfect,' said Stipe.

He'd glanced along the line. Had that strange feeling again.

'Who's the woman there?' he said. 'The one who's just looking at the birds?'

'I don't know her,' said the girl, without looking, though she knew who he was talking about. 'She's a friend of Connor's. Visiting from down in England somewhere, just along for the ride. What d'you think of the coffee?'

'Decent,' said Stipe.

'Right? I got sucked in by the marketing. It's a Christmas blend. You should be tasting the distilled essence of Bing Crosby.'

She laughed lightly, and he laughed along with her. A look between them, steam rising from warm cups, and then they turned together to the bay, and the sea of wildfowl.

The same clamour as before, the same rush of birds to the sky, starkly beautiful against the lightening grey of the morning clouds.

'You know geese?' she said.

It seemed that now they'd started talking, she wanted to make the most of it.

'Not at all,' said Stipe. 'Just like looking at them.'

'Yeah, I get that,' she said. 'It's magical.' A pause, but he knew it would be no more than that. He had the self-awareness to recognise that he had stood apart from the woman in the Vera hat in case she spoke to him, but he was happy to get into conversation with the young, beautiful woman in the beanie.

You're no different from anyone else, he thought, *despite protestations to the contrary.*

'The bulk of them are pink-footed, but you also get barnacle geese and snow geese. And greylag, of course. Some white-fronted, and some bean.'

'Bean geese?'

'Sure.'

'Never heard of them.'

'Well, they're a goose, all right,' she said.

'Don't you get better pictures on the other side of the bay?' he asked. 'Closer up.'

'Sure,' she said, 'but it's not quite as convenient, and we've all done that already this season. So, we're here today instead. Maybe this lot'll be back there tomorrow. They move around.'

'Not you?'

'Going back to Aberdeen this afternoon. Doing bird migration for my Masters dissertation. Spent a couple of days in Elgin, thought I'd come out with the bird geeks. Nice to have company. What's your excuse?'

'Live just around the corner. Like to come down here every now and again. Just for the view. Nothing scientific.' A pause. 'I also come when there aren't so many birds. It's quieter.'

'I'll bet,' she said. 'You go to work?'

'Copywriter,' he said. 'I work at home.'

'Nice. What does a copywriter do?'

He'd been asked that question many times. His favourite answer was a glib 'write copy', but that, sadly for him, was never the end of the conversation. So he'd stopped being glib.

'The dull part of the job is like, I don't know, writing really boring trade catalogues, that kind of thing. The fascinating history of a removals company in the north of England, or a newsletter on why your local water company is single-handedly saving the planet. So, everything from that, to writing *citrusy on the nose, with hints of langoustine on the pallet, drink with shell fish or on its own* on the back of a bottle of wine.'

She laughed.

'How many bottles of wine have you copy written?'

'None, though I did once blurb a local brewery, from which they extracted the marketing phrase *Drink With Everything*.'

'Genius.'

'Not really.'

'Well, that sounds like a cool job. What're you working on today?'

'Nothing on this week. Got a big contract starting on Monday, though, so we're cool.'

'You want to have breakfast?'

'Eh…'

'We can just go to your place. Wait, you live alone?'

'Sure.'

'Cool. You have food in or do we need to find a shop?'

She was young and she was beautiful, and the Walter Mitty in him had been in this position many times, yet it still felt like being run over by a train.

'There's eggs. Toast.' A beat. 'Coffee.'

'Sounds like breakfast,' she said, smiling. 'Let me get my shit together.'

4

Ellen

That night they slept in the same bed. They hadn't spoken to each other again after she'd hit him. Hadn't been in the same room until they met again in the bedroom.

I'm not giving up my damned bed for him, she thought. He can sleep in the spare room. And then he'd walked into the room, gone to the en suite to use the toilet and brush his teeth, and then he'd put on his pyjama bottoms and got into bed beside her.

He had two plasters making a cross on his face. Indeed, he'd placed them so that they made the shape of a Christian cross, rather than the familiar x-shape of crossing plasters, and this only added to her contempt.

His hurt that she should be annoyed; his search for absolution; the plasters; now lying silently in bed as though she should be able to stand it; each of them an annoyance that burrowed beneath her skin to distract her from the real hurt. He'd been having an affair, and she'd had no idea. They'd still had sex, they'd still laughed, they'd argued on occasion, but no more nor less than they had twenty-nine years previously, they'd talked about work, they'd shared stories. There being no such thing as a perfect couple, they had seemed to her, had she given it any thought, as near as dammit to the unachievable ideal.

And now, here she was lying in bed, in the same position where three nights previously she'd lain as they'd had sex, and she had orgasmed, and she not been the first woman to have an orgasm with him that day, and the thought made her sick.

The lights were off, they lay awake in the dark. The curtains were not thick, but there were no streetlights at this side of the house, trees and a park beyond, the night was cloudy, the moon invisible. A dark, dark night, the bedroom still, the house quiet. The sound of his breathing, the horror of worthlessness in her throat.

She dreaded him touching her, even a slight bump in the night, but she did not want to get out of bed. How dare he lie there? Yet if they fell asleep, as surely they would at some point, they might find themselves waking up entwined, or at least an arm draped across an inert body. The thought of it, of waking up like that, that first second, two seconds, three seconds, before the awareness of the new reality had kicked in, and then it would come thundering back, and she might be pressed against him, and the very idea of it had her stomach curling up, the taste of vomit in her throat.

'Can I hold you?'

The words appeared in the dark. He sounded weak. She felt every muscle in her body tighten. Clenched her fists, her skin prickled, went cold. She moved her right hand closer to herself, in beneath her body, so that he couldn't lightly touch it with his fingers.

'I forgive you,' he said. 'I know you were upset.'

She got up quickly, didn't turn to look at him, hardly needed to worry about bumping into anything as she walked quickly across the room, then she was out into the landing, slamming the door behind her.

5

Stipe

'You want to have sex?'

They'd got in from the shore. Jackets hung up, he put some music on, he'd made coffee for her and tea for himself, and made toast and scrambled eggs. Conversation was easy, and out of her duffel coat and hat, she was no less beautiful. They didn't yet know each other's names, but they quite liked that. It seemed to fit the narrative of the morning.

Nevertheless, the sex question had been out of the blue.

'Really?' was all he could think to say.

He'd thought he was getting on top of the morning, but perhaps not as well as he'd believed.

'Why not? I thought you were Walter Mitty? Don't you have casual sex with gorgeous women in these fantasies of yours?'

'Suppose I do,' said Stipe.

'I mean you're kind of hot, you have an attractive naivety about you, you make decent scrambled eggs,' and she laughed, 'and you listen to this weird 1920s music that, like, no one your age listens to anymore.'

'It's from the 50s,' he said, although he didn't object to the exaggeration of his singular place amongst thirty-three year-old music listeners.

'Nice. Who is it?'

'Hoagy Carmichael,' he said.

'Don't know him, but I kind of like the vibe. What's this one called?'

'*Ole Buttermilk Sky.*'

'Hmm. *Ole Buttermilk Sky*. That's got a ring to it. So, how about the sex?'

Stipe lifted the mug to his face, a familiar distraction method to both of them, drained the dregs, as that was all that remained, then placed the mug back on the table.

'I haven't had a shower,' he said.

She giggled.

'Really?'

'I just got up and went out to see the geese. Thought I'd have a shower when I got home.'

'Have you always had a shower in your fantasy sex?'

'Pretty much,' he said seriously, and she smiled.

'OK, so is it a showstopper, or do you want to go and have a shower and I'll wait?'

He stared blankly at her across the table. He imagined kissing her lips, his lips moving down to her neck, across her body.

'I've had a shower,' she said, 'you know, just in case you were worried.' She looked at her watch. 'Like, just a couple of hours ago. Is that recently enough?'

Finally Stipe smiled, and for the first time in a while his face relaxed.

'I'll go and have a shower,' he said. 'Give me a couple of minutes.'

* * *

They were sitting up in bed, like they were watching television, but they were just staring out of the window at a grey sky. Sex over. Hoagy Carmichael was still playing, on a loop, in the other room. The bedroom was cold, and they each had the duvet cover pulled up to their necks.

He'd emerged from the shower to find her still sitting at the kitchen table, coffee cup in hand, waiting. With practicality, he'd thought to mention he didn't have any condoms, and she'd said she was on the pill, and he'd said that wasn't the only reason to use a condom, and they'd nodded together, and made the silent agreement that millions of couples make around the world every day; I'll risk it if you risk it.

'I think I like this music,' she said, breaking a long silence. 'What'd you say his name was again?'

'Hoagy Carmichael.'

'Hoagy. What's that short for?'

'Hoagland.'

'He was called Hoagland?'

'That was his name, but I guess everyone called him Hoagy all his life.'

'Still, pretty weird to call your kid Hoagland. I've never heard of *that* before.'

'He was named after a circus troupe. The Hoaglands.'

'You've got the inside scoop.'

‘I looked it up on Wikipedia.’

‘Nice. Maybe I’ll get one of his CDs.’

‘Go for Hoagy Sings Carmichael, with the Pacific Jazz Men. That’s the best.’

‘Hmm, what are the odds of me remembering that?’

‘I’ll send you a text,’ he said.

‘Hmm…’

The clouds had formed a perfect sheet of grey, almost impossible to identify contours and depth. From where they were they couldn’t see much else bar the branches of a rowan tree that had already surrendered to winter.

‘What?’ asked Stipe.

‘Probably best you don’t text,’ she said. ‘I’m back in Aberdeen this afternoon, and Jason would be pissed if he thought I was getting random texts from some guy about music. Come to think of it, if I turn up and start listening to some centuries-old jazz guy no one’s ever heard of before, he’s going to think that’s a bit suspicious, right?’

‘Jason?’

‘My fiancé.’

A beat. Outside a crow flew across their line of vision.

‘I never said,’ she added after a few moments. ‘I decided it was my call to make, rather than yours. My problem.’

‘Not if Jason kills me,’ said Stipe, although without any self-pity. He wasn’t really worried about being killed by Jason.

‘Jason gets pissy,’ she said, ‘but he wouldn’t hit anyone, don’t worry. Anyway, he’s not going to find out.’

‘When are you getting married?’

‘In a month.’

Stipe blinked, glanced at her, then looked back at the grey sky.

‘Kinda soon, right?’

‘Yes,’ he said.

A beat. Another crow. And then it was gone, and there were no more crows. In the far distance, a pair of gulls.

‘Yep, I suppose you’re right,’ she said, even though he hadn’t expressed an opinion. ‘Kind of a last hurrah for me. I know I shouldn’t have, but here we are. No going back.’

Stipe thought to ask if he was a one-off, but the question never really got anywhere near delivery. He didn’t expect it would be, and he didn’t care anyway. Sex with a stranger might have been out of his comfort zone, but it wasn’t like it hadn’t been fun.

'I should probably be heading off,' she said. 'You mind if I dive in the shower?'

A beat. Stipe regarded the day ahead, and decided that it might not be too bad.

'Mind your head,' he said, and she giggled and rolled her eyes.

6

Ellen

She'd got on a train and headed north, and now she was sitting at a kitchen table with a mug of tea that was still too hot to drink, staring at the rising steam.

Her first port of call, having left home the morning after the evening before, had been her sister's. Janine had, unsurprisingly, spent the day spewing sympathy, looking at her sister as though she'd just received a terminal cancer diagnosis. Ellen had spent one night, then fled that morning after breakfast. Since her presence in her sister's family home – husband working at the Barbican, four kids at private school, hockey games and rugby matches and homework and drama lessons – promised to be something of a succubus, though no one said anything, everyone was happy to see her go. Easier that way. Nevertheless, no one was happier than Ellen.

'Too soon to look for the positives?' asked Connor.

Ellen's best friend from university. Her name wasn't Connor, but during freshers week, she'd got into a bar fight, laid out three guys in under a minute, someone had said it was like she was straight out a Terminator movie, and someone else had called her Sarah Connor. Sarah had been quickly dropped, Connor had stuck.

'Go on,' said Ellen, though her voice did not display much enthusiasm.

'There's all the sex you can get now.'

Ellen stared blankly across the table. There was music playing. A Paul McCartney album from some time in the previous thirty years, one of those that got lost along the way, the quality of the songs redundant when set against the fact they hadn't been recorded by the Beatles.

'Look at me,' said Ellen. 'I'm fifty-three. No one wants to have sex with fifty-three year-old women.'

'I've had lots of sex this year,' said Connor. 'You know this, because I always tell you about it.'

'You're still gorgeous. I was never gorgeous.'

'You're sexy as fuck, Ell, and you always have been. Giving yourself to David wasn't necessarily a bad move – and you understand, I'm not going to slag him off and say things like *I always thought he was a dick*, just in case the phone rings and you're back together by the end of the evening, but it doesn't mean I didn't always think he was a dick…'

'I know!'

'So the marriage wasn't necessarily a bad move, and as a result you did get to meet Alan Rickman and Emma Thompson, which was pretty cool, even though you were naïve enough to not try to sleep with either of them, but it's meant you've been hidden away from humankind all these years. This raw sex beast, unable to be unleashed.'

Having already been laughing ruefully at the Rickman remark – that the highlights of her marriage could be reduced to meeting a couple of movie stars – she laughed more loudly at being described as a raw sex beast.

'God, look at me,' she said again. 'And you know what, having spent the last two years of my marriage with my husband clearly not happy with what he was getting from me, it hardly fills me with confidence to get back out there, does it?'

'That's why you're here, darling,' said Connor. 'If you truly wanted to feel sorry for yourself, you'd have stayed at Janine's house until you'd shrivelled up into a horrible ball of despondency. But deep down you need freedom, you need liberation, so you fled. And you came here. And the first day of the rest of your sex life starts now.'

Ellen puffed out her cheeks, took another drink of tea, felt the deflation and the humiliation and the hurt come rushing in, laid the mug back on the table, and rested her forehead in her left hand, her forefinger worrying her brow.

Recognising the moment, Connor reached across and squeezed her other hand. They didn't look at each other. Eye contact at that moment would not have gone well.

'I haven't eaten anything yet,' said Ellen. 'I think that was what made it worse at Janine's place. She actually said I was already becoming anorexic. But the thought of food… how can you eat when someone's reached down you throat and ripped out your stomach?' A beat. In the background Sir Paul launched into a chirpy little song that would not have been out of place on the White album, but which had been written twenty-five years too late for immortality. 'I feel useless. Utterly useless. And… I know it's not about me.'

'It's really not.'

'I know. It's about him, and it's about, I don't know… it's about him being unable to deny attraction, it's him thinking there's some grand romantic ideal out there that can't be ignored, it's about him needing to recapture something, it's about him getting bored, it's about him being an asshole, it's about him being narcissistic, it's about him being a fucking wastrel piece of shit cunt fucking bellend spunk-pumpkin…'

The rising anger dissolved into laughter, Connor laughing along with her, and then the laughter died away and they were able to look at each other and smile, and then Ellen was staring at the table and the hurt was still there and the pain had not lessened.

'Fuck,' was all she was able to say at the end of it.

'Right,' said Connor, 'you may not be able to eat, but you can drink, clearly. Time to open the wine.'

'Yes, wine. More than happy to get hammered.'

'We have to be up at six tomorrow, so take that into consideration,' said Connor, opening the fridge door.

'Six?'

'We're going to look at the geese. It's fun. I can introduce you to a couple of the men.'

Ellen downed her tea, and set the mug on the table.

'Bring me wine, barkeep,' she said.

7

Stipe

The following day. Even though he knew he wasn't going to see the girl, Stipe still took a shower before heading out in the morning. Radio 3 on in the kitchen, he made coffee, warmed the milk, filled the McLaren thermos mug. Jacket, beanie, gloves, and he walked through the town to the sound of the awakening geese, past the Crown & Anchor, to the dual piers on the waterfront.

There were two dog walkers, a middle-aged couple walking hand in hand, and the woman in the Vera hat standing at the edge of the right-hand pier, presumably watching over her husband taking his morning swim. That was it for people on the piers.

He stood for a moment at the bottom of the slope looking out over the bay. He didn't see the geese, he just saw the absence of the photographers.

The girl had said there were members of their group out most mornings during the autumnal migration, but that they moved to different points of the bay. Today they were likely to be found on the other side, near the shallows, at the end of the small road down past Invererne. It was much too far away from where he currently stood to see if there was anyone there.

He'd hoped they'd be here instead, as though he could have willed them to come to the harbour, rather than the distant shallows. Now he contemplated the possibility of going there. He'd have to ride his bike. It would be at least half an hour, and to what end?

He dithered. He took a drink of coffee. He looked out over the bay, for the first time that morning really noticing the geese, no less abundant than they'd been the previous day. Pink footed and barnacle, snow and greylag. Canadian? He couldn't recall if the girl had said anything about Canadian geese.

He walked to the bottom of the slope, and then out along the opposite pier from the woman with the Vera hat. Still thinking about getting on his bike, and riding round the bay, knowing he wasn't going to do it. Nowhere near impulsive enough. He'd have had to think ahead, it would've had to have been an option when he went to bed the previous evening.

Unexpectedly sleeping with the girl hadn't been too far removed from the norm. It had started with walking down to the front, had been followed with going back to his own house, eating breakfast at his own table, and then going to his own bed. If she'd asked him back to her place, none of it would have happened.

And now the exceptional thing was getting on his bike and riding it around the bay when he hadn't been thinking about it, and he knew that wasn't going to happen.

'Tomorrow morning,' he said.

'Sorry?'

He turned. There was a woman looking at him. Red jacket, scarf around her neck, jeans. Mid-seventies maybe.

'What?' said Stipe.

'Sorry, I thought you said something about tomorrow.'

They stared at each other for a moment before Stipe finally shook his head, made himself think properly.

'Sorry, I was talking to myself.'

He smiled, hoped that would be the end of it. She rolled her eyes – at herself he presumed, rather than at him – touched his arm, apologised with a look and walked on.

He glanced at her back, and then turned to the geese, as more and more took flight for the morning.

Tomorrow morning, he thought. *Come back down, bring the bike, if they're not here, ride around the bay until you find them.*

He glanced after the woman in the red jacket, but she was now twenty yards away and did not appear to have been listening to his thoughts.

8

Ellen

She thought of flying away with the geese.

The previous day she had dragged herself out of bed at six as Connor had asked. She'd taken Connor's old camera, and she'd followed the small crowd to the pier to stand in the cold and watch the geese.

'This is Malcolm, one of the good guys,' Connor had said as an introduction to the first of the men. Malcolm had seemed nice enough, though no more interested in talking to Ellen than she'd been interested in talking to him.

'Yeah, I can see there's no spark,' Connor had said later. 'Too bad. Massive, massive cock.' And they'd dissolved into giggles, and laughter like that now ended by draining away into a well of sadness. Laughter was as alien as the idea of food. This moment did not deserve laughter.

That day, that first day at the bay, once Connor had gone to work, Ellen had sat at the window of the conservatory looking out over the water. Hour upon hour, a magazine unread in her lap. Never dozing off, never getting up, looking out on the grey bay, stretching away to the grey-green woods on the other side, which met the grey sky, here and there the flights of geese, in perfect and in ragtag Vs.

That night, more alcohol, this time tears, finally some food, though no more than cheese and biscuits, and then the following morning Connor was getting up early again to go to the other side of the bay. Going to bed, Ellen had said she wouldn't set an alarm. 'If I'm awake, I'll come with you.' She woke at some time after ten.

The day was grey again. She could hear the sound of birds through the open window. They seemed loud, and she wondered why the noise hadn't woken her earlier.

There was a picture of a face in her head. A young man she couldn't place. She'd seen him some time in the past couple of days, though he wasn't one of the geese photographic party.

She wondered what he was doing in her head. It didn't make sense. The thought of him was like the thought of a warm shower, or of Christmas in the Alps, or of Sunday lunch in autumn in a country pub.

Don't think about food. Don't think about alcohol.

She lay staring at the ceiling, the hollow shock in the pit of her stomach still there. She felt sick, though this morning it was more alcohol-related. She thought she should get up, but then couldn't bring herself to move, as moving was likely to lead to a mad dash to get to the bathroom in time, and so she closed her eyes, and when she opened them again it was already past midday.

* * *

At four-fifteen she got a text from David. **Are you OK? Worried about you.**

She didn't reply.

Ten minutes later, the follow-up. **I'm sorry, but I still care about you. Let me know you're all right.**

She didn't reply to that one either. She did, however, message both of her daughters, just so they'd know not to worry about her when their father got in touch.

* * *

'You're going again in the morning?'

Sitting at the table. Dinner. Less alcohol, more food. Thai-style fishcakes – neither Connor nor Ellen knew if Thais actually ever made fishcakes – rice with mushrooms and pine nuts, mashed green peas.

'I think so,' said Connor. 'I usually go out along the bay in the morning anyway, so I might as well meet up with the gang. And you know, Andrew might be there tomorrow.'

Ellen stared drily across the table. Connor had her eyebrows raised in expectation, willing her to ask.

'Go on, then,' said Ellen.

'Don't mock it,' said Connor laughing. 'He's gorgeous. Works down at Glenlivet. Something in sales. Travels a lot, and I mean, like food shows in the US and Japan and Australia. I think he's a bit of a thing in whisky.'

'Available is he?'

'Yes and no. If you know what I mean.'

Ellen smiled ruefully, shook her head.

'You're terrible.'

'Look, their three kids are at boarding school, and I mean, they're at Gordonstoun. So they're at boarding school like twenty minutes from the family home. Who does that?'

'Aren't they day boarders?'

'No! They like, go home every third weekend or something. And Andrew's wife doesn't work. So, what d'you think she does all day when he's on the other side of the planet, hmm?'

'God, you're awful. I mean, if he's a philanderer, don't you think I would have an innate sympathy with this woman, whoever she is? She and I are sisters.'

Connor rolled her eyes, knowing that Ellen hadn't meant it. She cared no more for Andrew's wife now than she had five minutes previously, when she'd been unaware of her existence.

'I'm introducing you to Andrew. He's fit, he's got a billion stories, and he likes older woman, so you're in.'

'What age is he?'

'Forty. Thereabouts.'

'Jesus, he won't even know I exist.'

Connor took a drink, cut a piece of fishcake, put it into her mouth. Smiled.

'He noticed me,' she said.

9

Stipe

No coffee in hand, or anywhere else about his person – Stipe wasn't great at multi-tasking – he rode his bike through the streets, past the Crown & Anchor, and down to the pier side.

There were the dog walkers, and there was the woman in the Vera hat, and there was the photography club, or the bird watching club, or whatever kind of club they were. A line of cameras on tripods along the pier, aiming out over the bay, or up to the sky.

He saw her straight away. The completely illogical woman who had got under his skin. *Illogical woman?* That didn't make sense. It was illogical that she'd got under his skin, but she herself was not illogical. Whatever she was, she was one woman, and he saw her before he saw twenty thousand geese.

He was emboldened coming here because of the girl. He lived his life encased in two protective layers. The first his imagination, taking him to distant worlds and shielding him from this one; the other his natural reserve, born of a lack of confidence. It was the latter that had been shattered by the girl. She'd been bold and confident and quite unlike anyone else he had in his life, she was beautiful and she'd wanted him, she'd had him, and she'd left, leaving behind an unexpected feeling of liberation, and an innate confidence. That the latter would likely not last meant little at that moment. A crisp, fresh morning in November, looking out on a pier, where there was a woman in amongst a group of photographers, and he was attracted to her in a way he didn't understand.

He'd thought about her when making love to the girl. Funny. And *the girl*? Really? That was how he was thinking of the twenty-five year-old woman he'd slept with. *The girl*. Like he was in the nineteen fifties. But that was the word that settled in his head, particularly next to this woman on the pier.

When he'd seen her two days previously, she'd been standing alone. She was obviously with this group of birdwatchers, but there was something detached about her. She was with them, but not one of them. And when thinking about her this morning, that was how he'd imagined it was going to be again.

And there she was, not photographing the birds. Maybe she didn't even have a camera with her. But this morning, she was not alone. All the others were bent to their cameras, except one man who was standing chatting with the woman. Eye contact, smiling, a laugh, a self-conscious rub of the chin, and she was laughing with him.

There had been no Walter Mitty imaginings about her, though. He had no idea why he was drawn to her, so he had no idea what he wanted to happen as a result of speaking to her. And so finding her in potentially intimate conversation with another man – the awfulness of the shared laughter – did not trample over some ideal meeting he had planned. He had nothing planned.

He watched her for a few moments. Birds all around, though he did not yet hear or see them. The chill of morning, the barking of a dog, the splash of a middle-aged man in cold water, while his wife in a Vera hat watched over him. Perhaps he was a heart attack risk. Stipe noticed none of it.

Disappointment seeped in, the feeling with which the fantasist is familiar.

In this particular fantasy he had allowed himself to believe there was some strange higher force at work. He had seen this woman once, briefly, and she'd got under his skin. He had dreamt about her that night – he knew it from the way he was thinking about her when he'd woken, though he couldn't remember the dream – and he had known with certainty she would be on the pier this morning.

And she was. And she was with another man. Older, more confident, a look of quality about him. Quality? Which quality?

'Not one of the qualities,' he said, 'just quality itself.'

'Sorry?'

Distracted, Stipe turned.

'What?'

They stared at each other for a moment, a curious look. The same woman from the previous morning.

'You're talking to yourself again, aren't you?'

Stipe did not answer. The dreamer extracted rudely from the dream is often disorientated.

'I won't say we've got to stop meeting like this,' she said, and once again she touched his arm. 'Such a cliché. Perhaps I'll see you tomorrow morning nevertheless.'

She smiled warmly, Stipe finally managed to pull himself into the moment to return the smile, and she walked on her way.

A beat, one, two, aware of the sound of a gull on the roof of the building next to him, then he turned back to the pier. In a story, she would have been looking at him.

She was laughing, and the man, the businessman with an air of elegant sophistication, was touching her arm, laughing with her.

'There goes that,' he said softly, then found himself turning to see if he'd been overheard.

A shake of the head, and then he turned away from the piers and the bay, had had not so much as noticed a goose, despite their prodigious number, and then he stood up on his bike and rode up the small hill towards the inn.

The ululation of the gulls, the cacophonous honking of the geese, the awakening of the day against familiar low cloud, and the sound of the waves upon the shore. A second or two after he was gone, Ellen looked away from Andrew, the elegant sophisticate, to the road that ran along the shore. Stipe was gone, but she felt his absence as she looked at the space where he'd been.

10

Ellen & Stipe

She was sitting on a bench at the end of the path that runs along the front of the town, past the boat yard, where the land turns east to create the narrow mouth of the bay. She'd been over the dunes, down onto the beach, to look out on the waves of the Moray Firth, the green hills of Sutherland in the distance, then she'd followed the rush of the water through the narrow funnel back round, and now she was sitting alone on a bench, watching the world. The sea and the birds, the trees of Culbin forest a shuffling crowd in the wind.

How long could she stay here? Not that there was much to get back to. Working part time in the Oxfam shop on High Street, the course in digital music production at the local college. Shopping and cooking and looking after the house. Dinner on the table for David. She wouldn't be doing that again.

It wasn't that she had anything to get back to, but here, staying with Connor, she was living someone else's life. Getting up at 6 am to look at geese, talking to men that Connor thought suitable, for all the world like she was Mrs Bennet, and she had the annual income of all the men in the area marked on a linear graph against availability.

This was what she was facing now. She'd had the punch in the stomach. She hadn't remotely begun to come to terms with it, but the question of the day still sat there in front of her, like it was a giant bird floating on the water, ten yards offshore.

What next?

Now the heartache, now the pain of rejection, now the feelings of worthlessness, now the anger, and now the visceral torture, the insidious cancer of uselessness eating away inside.

So much for now. Indeed, what next?

There was a movement beside her as someone sat on the bench. She didn't immediately look, although she knew who it was. She felt him. Her brow furrowed.

Stipe didn't look at her either. They sat together, staring out across the water, their eyes on the same point in the midst of the trees in the forest.

He'd come out for a walk. Late morning. Had thought of riding his bike round the bay, going into the forest. Instead, had gone for his regular expedition. Down by the bay, cut to the narrow entrance, over the dunes, down to the beach, along the coast to Burghead, turn back inland for the walk home on the small country roads.

His thinking walk, when he often formulated project outlines, or thought of the next snappy one-liner to go at the top of the flyer to be posted through ten thousand letterboxes in the area, before being transferred directly to the recycling.

What had he had to think about today?

In the seven minutes it had taken him to get from his house to this point, he'd thought about the woman he was now sitting next to. He had not thought what he would say if he met her, as he hadn't thought he would. His new-found confidence had at least allowed him to sit down, but words would not yet come.

A moment of uncertainty quickly gave away to a feeling of ease. That this, strangely, was something that was supposed to happen. They were meant to be sitting next to each other, at this moment, in this spot, looking out on this bay, and these birds, and the beach, and the woods.

Words found him.

'There's an old song,' he began, the words appearing on his lips. 'Peter Gabriel. Flying birds, excellent birds, something like that? I don't even remember what it was called, but I've had it in my head for weeks now. Every time I come down here. Flying birds, excellent birds…'

'*This Is The Picture*,' she said. They still didn't look at each other, but he could tell she was smiling.

'My parents gave me the album because it was number one in the charts when I was born,' he said. A beat. 'That's pretty cheesy.'

She didn't immediately respond, and finally he turned to look at her. First time, up close. She was staring at him, amused, curious.

'Well, that's funny,' she said.

She had a lovely smile. Warm. Honest.

'You think?'

'I did a year at college, then I was going to be a sound engineer in records. Had it all planned out. Got a trainee position at Townhouse Studio. Everyone was using it then. Everyone. You know the drums on *In The Air Tonight*?'

'Of course.'

'They were recorded there, and it became the place to be. So, one of the first things I worked on – and when I say worked, I sat at the back of the room watching, while occasionally nipping out to make tea – was that Gabriel album. That song was Laurie Anderson's, and he added to it. Funny song.'

'Wow.'

'I suppose.'

'What was Peter Gabriel like? They say he's decent.'

'Never met him.'

'Oh. Did you work on anything else interesting?'

'Some, I suppose, but nothing super-interesting. Plenty of time for that. I'll tell you later.'

They looked curiously at each other, because they'd only just met, yet they both knew there'd be a later.

'Then I met David, and I was going to have a great career and he was going to have a great career, then I got pregnant, and I got pregnant again, and I ended up not having a career at all, and David… well, he's done all right, I suppose.' A beat, wondering if she'd said too much but knowing, really, that she hadn't, as Stipe wasn't the kind of person to whom she *could* say too much, and then the words, 'Who was the girl?' appeared on her lips from nowhere.

A beat. Silence to the cry of the gulls.

'Don't you know her?' said Stipe. 'She was part of your group.'

'I'm just up here staying with a friend. Connor. She was mostly interested in introducing me to the men. That girl wasn't there today.'

'She went back through to Aberdeen. I only met her that morning. Won't see her again. Getting married in a month.'

'You sleep with her?'

'Yep.'

'How was that?'

'All right.'

Ellen nodded.

When was the last time she'd found someone this easy to speak to?

'What about you?'

A moment, then she glanced at him with, 'How d'you mean?'

'You were talking to a guy this morning.'

'Hmm,' she said. 'I didn't see you.'

‘I came to speak to you, but you seemed occupied.’

‘Oh, well don’t worry about him.’ Funny use of the word worry, which they both noticed. ‘Name’s Andrew. Connor thought we were a perfect match. For sex, I mean, not long term.’

‘And did you?’

‘Nope. Didn’t like the cut of his jib.’

Silence. She glanced at him again, noticed he was stopping himself saying something.

‘We appear to be getting it all out there right from the off,’ she said, ‘so you might as well say it. I have literally no idea what’s happening here, so there’s no judgement being made.’

‘I was going to say you looked like you were enjoying his company, but I stopped myself because I didn’t want you to think that I was either, a) jealous and sad, because I was neither, or b) following you like a deranged serial killer.’

She laughed.

‘Maybe I *was* a bit jealous. I shouldn’t say I wasn’t. That’s what people always say in movies, even though everyone knows they’re jealous. Like we’re all conditioned to deny it.’

‘That’s OK, no judgement, like I said. And, no, there was nothing there. I mean, he was nice enough, and he was funny, I suppose, but God, he’s in love with himself. I didn’t want to be added to his list. Though, to be fair to the man, I suspect he didn’t actually want to add me to his list in the first place. Way too old for him.’

Those words hung out there, but there was an instant openness between them, so they did not hang awkwardly.

‘Which doesn’t explain you,’ she said.

‘No.’

Silence briefly returned, the shanty silence of the seaside, but it did not last.

‘You live here?’ she asked.

‘Five years now. Work from home. I’m a copywriter.’

‘Nice,’ she said. ‘I live in Camberwell. Found out five days ago my husband was sleeping with Jan. That’s Jan in make-up, not Jan in sound, in case you were wondering.’ He smiled. ‘I came here to get away, but I’ve no idea what’s going to happen now. I was sitting here thinking about the future. Wondering what it was going to look like. I really have no idea.’ A beat. ‘Then you sat down.’

He nodded. They still hadn’t looked at each other again, yet they both felt it. The warmth of early afternoon.

'It's gone twelve,' he said. 'How about lunch?'

She smiled, nodded to the movement of her lips.

'Sounds like a nice start to the future,' she said.

With perfect timing, they both moved their hands, and then they touched, they felt the exhilaration of it, then their fingers slipped together and entangled.

Above them, in an imperfect V formation, a hundred and three geese headed out to sea.

The Artist

It had been twenty-five years since the movie opposite Bruce Willis. His screen time hadn't been great, but he'd been the perfect villain. Then he'd taken the role with Bobby De Niro that the critics had admired but which no one had watched, following which he'd jumped at the part in the Mel Gibson film just as people had stopped going to see Mel Gibson. From then on the slide had been precipitous, every step he took seemingly the wrong one. Having failed to get the part of Snape in Harry Potter he had stupidly followed his agent's advice and refused to accept a lesser role. When he'd returned to the producers a few years later, crawling and desperate behind a new agent, he hadn't even been given an audition for the role of Slughorn.

'All right! Can we have some quiet, please?' shouted the Assistant Director.

The noise died away. Someone laughed loudly, then cut it short. The low hum of filmmakers at work settled over the production. Such as it was.

There had been some television work on Channel 4, and of course a regular place on *Casualty* whenever he'd wanted it. But he loved film. He needed to be in film. He wanted his Hollywood star, and he wasn't going to get that playing an ageing, racist, homosexual Polish doctor on BBC1 at 8pm on a Saturday.

Not that he was likely to get it here either.

'OK, let's keep it together, people,' said the AD, his voice quieter now. 'Scene Twelve, Take One.'

As far as anyone knew, the director was currently engaged with the best boy in one of the three caravans parked outside the old manor house.

The large wooden door opened, a young woman entered. She immediately gasped, her hand going to her mouth in affected surprise.

'Like, Marvin, what are you doing? That's, like, totally gross and stuff!'

The other young woman looked up from the bed.

'Bliss, help me!' she panted. 'Marvin isn't a priest, he's a vampire zombie! And he's not even from this planet!'

Bliss looked curiously at Marvin, who was leaning over the half-naked Summer, about to plunge his fangs into her breasts.

'Really?' said Bliss. 'That is, like, so weird. A vampire

zombie? Do I even know what that is?'

The vampire zombie turned, malice in his eyes. The same look of evil disdain with which he had once held sway over Bruce Willis.

'I am centuries old,' he said. 'I was born before time itself. I walk with the dead, angels and demons are my companions...' He hesitated. The AD sat forward. One take per scene was pretty much all they could afford. 'I...' he began again, but this time he stopped quickly, turned away from the naked breasts and straightened up.

'Cut!' shouted the AD. He breathed heavily, counted to five. 'What is it, George?'

'This,' said George, turning his back on the young woman who still lay naked on the bed, not feeling it necessary to cover herself. 'This is absurd.'

The AD held his gaze but did not speak.

'Bliss is right,' said George, indicating Bliss with a nod, but not actually looking at her.

'Like, duh...' said Bliss.

'Do any of us actually know what a vampire zombie even is?' said George.

'Can you just do the scene, please?'

'How can I possibly speak to my audience?'

'Your audience wants to see you suck blood from that girl's tits. End of. Now will you just do it?'

George turned away from the AD – albeit not in the direction of the tits – and tossed a theatrical hand in the air.

'The vampire is a sophisticate. His way is subtle and intelligent, guile and sophistry are his companions. But not the zombie. The zombie is quite the opposite. Base and ignoble, brutish, driven by a slavish lust for flesh. With the exception of the blessed Colin Firth, is there an actor among us who could reconcile the two?'

The AD scratched his ear and leaned forward.

'George. This isn't *Pericles, Vampire Zombie of Tyre*, or, I don't know, *The Merry Vampire Zombies of Windsor*. It's a low budget horror, porn, slasher, noir, screwball comedy. Our audience doesn't want sophistry. They think sophistry is the art of arranging cushions.'

George straightened his shoulders. He'd started this argument many times in his head, and now, here he was at last, in its midst. Time to engage.

'I get letters from my fans. Letters, not e-mails or Tweets. My fans are people of quality. And they tell me that what they look for in my films is a certain finesse, that rare urbanity and savoir-faire one so rarely sees these days.'

The AD was still scratching his ear. He sucked his lips for a second and then indicated with his hand for Bobby, the unpaid script editor who was hanging around the set learning the ropes, to come over. He jogged up, glad to have something to do. A moment of excited fear, wondering if the AD was going to request a last-second dialogue addition.

'Bobby', said the AD, 'can you remind George of the title of the film we're making here today.'

Having, in the space of three seconds, decided that he was about to be asked to contribute some hastily written dialogue for the RSC-trained thespian star of the movie, Bobby was momentarily discombobulated. Everyone knew the name of the movie.

The AD prompted him with a pair of raised eyebrows.

'Sir,' said Bobby. 'It's *Butt-Naked Alien Vampire Zombies Go Jesus*.'

'Thanks, Bob,' said the AD, ushering him away with the reverse of the gesture with which he'd brought him forward.

Bobby retreated, the sudden burst of adrenaline having evaporated, returning wearily to his spot on the sidelines.

The AD looked back at George.

'*Butt-Naked Alien Vampire Zombies Go Jesus*,' he said. 'A title which seems to date from the Renaissance itself, doesn't it?'

When George conducted these arguments in his head, he was never greeted by sarcasm.

'I think, in fact, the writer maybe even borrowed the name from a Donatello sculpture. Am I right?' the AD added, looking around the small movie crew. There were a few laughs, although one or two of them came reluctantly. George might have been something of a pompous oaf, but he was likeable enough, and had interesting stories to tell of the world of studio movies, to which they all aspired.

'Nevertheless, George,' said the AD, having gloried in his small moment of mocking triumph, 'I'd be very grateful if you could do me the favour, on this occasion, of just biting the girl's tits. On camera. As written in the script, which you read before signing up to do the movie.'

They held the gaze across the short distance of the large

bedroom. Eighteenth century wood panelling on the walls, furnishing picked up from Freecycle two days earlier, rented film equipment due to be returned the day after tomorrow.

'Or do we need to have a chat with legal?'

George had heard that line before. George had heard that line from directors and producers who actually had a legal department to call upon. If this lot had a 'legal', it would likely be someone's cousin who was in their first year of law at Southampton.

George finally lowered his eyes, looking down from the lofty height of his straightened shoulders, and slowly the air left his chest, the fight faded away.

'You know,' said Bliss, 'I think my character should be more tangential.'

No one reacted.

'Like, a *lot* more tangential.'

* * *

That evening, George retired alone to his dingy little hotel room somewhere in the heart of old Somersetshire. The young lady whose breasts he'd feasted upon earlier in the day once more offered her breasts, this time in a more intimate setting, but he politely refused.

The following morning George did not come down for breakfast.

The Case Of The Stained Glass Widow (Redux)

(A DCI Jericho Story)

1

DCI Robert Jericho walked slowly up the short length of Wells High Street. A damp Wednesday morning in February. It had been a long, bleak and mild winter. Dull days, with not a hint of snow and barely any frost. Up ahead the midweek market was being set up in the city square, and the air was filled with the ringing of the Cathedral matins bells.

Jericho was walking with even more of a stoop than usual, having woken with a cricked neck. Before emerging like a hunchback out into the grey of morning, he had swallowed four pain killers and had rummaged through the cabinet in the bathroom – the contents of which had been moved wholesale from his house in London some years earlier, remaining untouched ever since – managing to dig up a Deep Heat aerosol which had gone out of date in 1995. He had sprayed it on his neck and back as best he could, which had given him the quality of the medicinal stench without helping his neck in any way.

He attracted a couple of glances from the market stalls, but Jericho generally wasn't the kind of man that people looked at in the street. He slipped by, invisible to most, blending in with whatever setting he happened to be walking slowly through at the time.

Which was odd for a man who remained the most famous detective in the country.

He walked through the arch at Penniless Porch, immediately seeing the object of his mission before him. As the bells rang out across Cathedral Green, a lone man stood before the great 13th century building. A placard in one hand, his other arm raised in anger, shaking his fist at Wells Cathedral as if the old structure was itself communicating.

'Bloody bells!' shouted the old man, his fist shaking. 'Shut the fuck up!'

Jericho hesitated while he took in the scene, and then moved forward at the same strolling pace at which he'd walked up the High Street. As he came alongside the old man, who was clean shaven, wearing a slightly bizarre long mauve raincoat and an old pair of black Wellingtons, the bells suddenly stopped, and this man, who'd been so forcefully haranguing the entire Church of England, stopped mid-rant and snorted.

‘’Bout bloody time,’ he muttered.

He turned as Jericho stopped beside him. ‘Bloody bells,’ he said, when he saw that Jericho had come to engage him. ‘What d’you want?’ he added sourly.

Jericho flashed his badge at the old man, who was already well aware of Jericho’s identity.

‘Professor Wittering,’ said Jericho, his voice weary, ‘you’ve been warned. This is the last time. Really. If you’re back here tomorrow, we’re bringing you in.’

‘Bloody bells,’ said Reginald Wittering. ‘Anyway, what are they doing sending a Chief Inspector? And a detective at that. This your punishment for smelling like a jockstrap?’

A couple of guys had called in sick. They’d been thin on the ground. Jericho had fancied the walk and said he’d take it. No other reason.

‘How long have you lived in Wells?’ said Jericho, ignoring the question.

Wittering knew where this line of questioning was leading.

‘Three years,’ he muttered in reply, giving Jericho a look of loathing.

Jericho nodded. He turned and indicated the Cathedral, then looked back at Wittering, wincing slightly at the movement.

‘Slept funny?’ asked Wittering, taking pleasure in the question.

‘Three years,’ said Jericho drily. ‘This lot, the Church, they got here a long time ago. They got here first. These bells have been ringing out over here for centuries. If you don’t like the sound of bells, go and live... God, I don’t know, in Pyongyang, or wherever…’

Wittering raised a miserable eyebrow, then looked back at the Cathedral. Which was when it started. What was to become known as the Case of the Stained Glass Widow.

As the two men looked at the Cathedral – as if expecting something to happen – something did. The small door at the front was flung open, and out ran a man in the long maroon tunic of a cathedral verger. He stopped on the grass outside the building and looked around at no one in particular. As it was, the only two people present on the green were Jericho and Wittering.

‘There’s been a murder!’ cried the verger loudly, his voice tinged with desperation. The words echoed out into the silence and the grey light of dawn of 7:27 on a weekday morning.

Jericho groaned.

'Hah!' barked Wittering, smiling broadly. 'That'll be why they sent a fucking detective.' Then, holding tightly onto his banner, he turned and started walking away from the Cathedral.

'For God's sake,' muttered Jericho darkly, and then, with another wince at his sore neck, he walked towards the Cathedral.

2

Matins had been cancelled, the crowd of seventeen filing slowly out into the grey morning, as dawn appeared mournfully over the city. Jericho had stood over the body in the Cathedral, ascertaining that murder had indeed been committed – the knife buried in the neck seemed confirmation in itself – and had put the call through to the station to raise the alarm. All hands required. It was time for the two constables who had called in sick to down the paracetamol and crawl into the office.

The body had been discovered in the Chapter House, a large, round room to the side of the Cathedral, up a wide flight of ancient and worn stairs. The pool of blood had spread wide, seeping into the stone floor. The stain would never be fully removed.

It was a little after nine. The Cathedral had been closed off, all other morning activities postponed. Jericho was standing outside, keeping an eye on the small crowd that had gathered at the exciting news. He could hear the sound of the school swing band coming from the old music department building adjacent to the Cathedral; he wasn't sure, but they seemed to be playing *We All Stand Together* from *Rupert & The Frog Song*, lending a slightly bizarre air to the murderous morning. A large majority of the gathered crowd – standing as if they might expect to see at the very least an action replay of the murder or, if things really picked up, a second killing – seemed to be made up of school children who'd elected to be late for their first lesson of the day.

With Jericho's Detective Sergeant, DS Haynes, on the south coast on a three-week course at MI6's Fort Monckton in Gosport, Jericho was currently being shadowed by a young Detective Constable named Krause, with whom Jericho had so little in common he'd begun to wonder if perhaps he and Krause were from a different species. More realistically, he didn't understand anyone who was thirty years younger than him, and it felt like more than one generation separated them.

'We've had ID confirmed, sir,' said Krause. 'They're just bagging up the body now. Jeffery Parks, fifty-seven, owned the old bookshop out on the Bath road. I thought I'd get out there now.'

‘Where’d you get that?’ asked Jericho.

Krause followed his eyes to the cup of coffee in his right hand.

‘Constable Walker. Think it’s from that new café just round on the square. Did you want one?’

‘Is there a wife?’ asked Jericho, ignoring the coffee question, even though he was the one who’d brought it up. ‘Well… widow.’

‘Seems to be. The guy we talked to, you know, he’s just some guy who works in there.’

‘A verger,’ said Jericho.

‘Yeah, verger. Knew Parks a bit. Says he was married, but didn't know much about them.’

‘We’ll go to his house first,’ said Jericho. ‘Then the shop.’

He started to walk off in the direction of the market square and then stopped, Krause on his heels.

‘Where are we going?’ asked Jericho. ‘I presume you’ve got an address.’

‘This is right,’ said Krause. ‘We’ll get the coffee on the way.’

* * *

There was nobody home. There weren’t many places in Wells more than a fifteen minute walk from the Cathedral, although it turned out that Parks’s house was at the far end of the town, on the Burcott road beyond the fire station, in the opposite direction from the book shop where he’d worked.

‘Will I get a car to come and pick us up?’ asked Krause, as they turned away from the house and started walking back towards the centre of town.

‘We’ll walk,’ said Jericho. ‘It’s good for you.’

They walked on in silence. Jericho finished his coffee and tossed the cup into a bin, wiped his lips with the sleeve of his coat. He was aware that Krause was casting glances at him, waiting for him to do something. Something to dramatically take the lead in the investigation.

Jericho had come to Wells to disappear, to lose his reputation in a quiet backwater where nothing much ever happened. There were worse reputations to have than the one with which he’d been landed, but it still annoyed him. He didn’t want anyone having expectations of him.

‘What?’ said Jericho eventually.

They were passing St Cuthbert's church, where once a man's head had exploded, impaled by falling masonry, in the movie *Hot Fuzz*.

'Just, you know,' began Krause uncertainly. 'What d'you think? Of the murder?'

Krause was twenty-five, and a good six inches taller than Jericho, and Jericho's natural stoop made him seem even taller.

'What makes you think I think anything?'

'It's what you do,' said Krause. 'You've never failed to solve a crime. The papers say you've always got the killer pegged in the first five minutes of the investigation.'

'The papers are full of crap, son,' said Jericho. 'Make any sort of decision in the first five minutes and you're going to prejudice the process of the entire investigation. Contrary to what the papers say, you should keep your mind open right up until the point you have concrete proof.'

Krause nodded, a look on his face like he was mentally writing it down, perhaps so he could put it on Twitter or Instagram. Jericho briefly imagined Krause standing, smiling, over a corpse, giving a thumbs up, taking a selfie, accompanied by an inspirational quote gleaned from the senior detective.

'Even then,' said Jericho, 'remember that if it gets hot enough, concrete melts.'

'You think?' said Krause. 'Doesn't it break into its constituent parts and go on fire and evaporate, or carbonise, something like that?'

Jericho gave him a sideways glance, then said, 'Look, the papers say whatever helps sell, whatever sounds like a good story.' He paused, but had momentarily found his voice. 'Everyone knows that, everyone knows they just make shit up and bend facts to fit the story they want to print, and yet, *and yet*, people still believe what they read. Isn't it weird?'

Krause glanced round, down really, wondering if he was supposed to answer.

'*Middle-aged detective continues to get lucky*,' said Jericho. 'That's not a story. No one cares. However, *modern day Sherlock Holmes nails another bastard with stroke of sleuthing genius*. *That's* a story. Who cares whether or not it's true?'

'So, you don't already know who did this?' asked Krause anyway.

'Of course I don't know. So far, who have we got? The guy who found the body? The widow who we haven't met? His work

colleagues, assuming there are some?'
'Well?' said Krause. 'Which one d'you think?'
Jericho gave him the resigned look of a tortured parent.
'The widow,' he said, eventually. 'It's the widow.'
Krause smiled. 'I'll hold you to it.'
Jericho rolled his eyes, and on they walked.

3

The shop was small and pleasantly old-fashioned. An independent bookshop, where books cost what they were supposed to cost and hadn't been reduced to £1.99, where the recommendations had been read by the staff and recommended because they were good, and not because the publisher had forked out £25,000 for the privilege, where novels mixed with travelogues and biographies of war-time pilots, and where there wasn't a hint of a book ghost-written on behalf of someone called Wayne or Katie or Cheryl. The whole place was so alien to what has become the norm, it was like walking into Narnia.

The small bell tinkled on the door as they entered. There were no customers. A small, attractive woman looked over the counter from behind heavy black-rimmed glasses. Her eyes were red, and Jericho wondered if she already knew.

They closed the door and paused for a moment to take in the surroundings.

'Are you Caroline?' asked Jericho.

'Caroline only comes in at the weekend,' said the woman, her voice sounding stronger than she looked. 'You'll get her on Saturday morning.'

'I just saw her name on a staff recommendation in the window,' said Jericho. 'You must be Ilsa?'

Krause smiled and shook his head, as if in awe of Jericho's observational genius.

Ilsa Ravenwood looked slightly confused, so Jericho held forward his ID card. Immediately, her hand went to her mouth, her whole chest seemed to shrink in on itself.

'Has something happened?' she asked, voice having instantly weakened.

'You're already worried about Mr Parks?'

'I was supposed to see him last night.'

'He's dead,' said Jericho bluntly. 'Someone stabbed him in the neck.'

She gasped, took a step backwards. A moment, while the men impotently waited to see if she would collapse, and then Krause moved around the counter, and took her arm. He glanced at Jericho, taken aback by his lack of compassion, although it wasn't as though he hadn't also been told about that part of the DCI's character.

'Maybe you should sit down,' said Krause, easing her back towards a small chair beside a desk.

Ilsa Ravenwood slumped down into the seat, her face crumpled in shock.

'Ilsa,' said Jericho. 'Like in *Casablanca*.'

* * *

It took twenty minutes before she was able to talk any further. After placing the *Closed* sign on the door, Krause made her a coffee and sat beside her saying what he presumed to be the right things, while Jericho perused the books. He liked the look of *The Closing of the Western Mind* by Charles Freeman, but thought it might be insensitive to offer to buy it.

Eventually, at a nod from Krause, Jericho came over and stood at the counter.

'Can I ask you a few questions, Mrs Ravenwood?' and she nodded. 'Can you tell us where we might find Mrs Parks?'

'Australia,' she said. 'She left last week to spend some time with her sister in Sydney.'

'How long was –'

'About a month.'

'And you and Mr Parks were using the opportunity of his wife's absence to further your affair?'

Ilsa Ravenwood stared at Jericho, and then finally crumpled forward, her head in her hands, sobbing bitterly.

* * *

They walked away from the shop half an hour later, leaving the bereft Mrs Ravenwood in the hands of a young police officer, trained in the modern arts of compassion, Krause finding that he was a little out of his depth.

'That was good,' said Krause, as they headed back in the direction of the Cathedral. 'You're good. Blunt. But good.'

Jericho stared straight ahead. He'd have preferred to have been conducting the investigation on his own, but this was where he was. He was babysitting a detective constable on the instruction of his superintendent, and there was nothing he could do about it.

‘Why?’ he asked.

‘You spot stuff. That thing about her having an affair. Very good.’

‘Are you being serious?’

They passed the lower end of Vicar’s Close, and could hear the random runs of a student practicing scales on a piccolo.

‘Sure. It was instinctive genius. That’s the kind of thing they talk about in the Sun.’

Jericho took a moment. Here it was again, the regular occurrence, the urge to shut down, to go and sit in a corner and drink coffee and not talk to anyone, sweeping over him.

‘She’d been crying,’ he said eventually. ‘She was obviously upset at him not being somewhere he should have been, and it wasn’t because he was late getting to work. We’ll find that he’s been dead since some time yesterday evening.’

‘Decent,’ said Krause. ‘Of course, you were wrong about the widow.’

Jericho paused, a momentary breaking of his stride, and then he picked up pace again.

‘For a kick-off,’ he said, ‘I didn’t say I thought it was the widow.’

‘Sure you did.’

‘I was being facetious. I had, and still have, no idea who did it. And secondly, let’s just establish that the widow is definitely in Australia before we go taking her off the slate, shall we? And let’s not rule out the possibility of her having an accomplice.’

Krause nodded, pulled his phone from his pocket.

‘I see what you’re doing there,’ he said. ‘Covering the angles. Very nice.’

‘Sure,’ said Jericho, ‘sometimes I amaze even myself. I’m going back to the Cathedral. You get down to the station and start making enquiries after the wife. If you get a number for her, wait until I get back and I’ll give her a call.’

‘Sir,’ said Krause, and he saluted and walked quickly away, past the dwindling crowd of curiosity.

4

Three hours later. Jericho was back at the station, sitting in his office, looking out over the fields stretching towards Glastonbury. Usually he could see the Tor; it didn't even have to be a good day. Today, however, the weather was so grim, so coldly claustrophobic, the hill was lost in the murk. It was lunchtime, he was hungry, his stomach was making strange noises, the painkillers were wearing off and his neck was beginning to hurt again. He was drinking his fifth coffee of the day.

The door opened, Krause appeared. Jericho didn't turn, just kept on staring across the fields. Krause came and stood beside him, looking at the view.

'I hate days like this,' said Krause. A beat, then he added, 'Soul-suckingly bleak.'

Jericho didn't respond. He wasn't disposed to get into what would likely be a flippant discussion with a detective constable who was doing little more than passing through. And if he got started on things that he hated, things that annoyed him, would he ever stop? Things about living in Britain, things about being a police officer, and just things about what happened to you from the moment you got out of bed.

He didn't want to be that person, but it had always been a part of him, and since Amanda had gone it had become unavoidably, and inescapably, all of him.

He turned, straightened – winced at the pain in his neck as he did so – and looked up at Krause.

'Tell me everything,' he said.

'Of course,' said Krause. 'We've established that the wife is definitely in Australia. She was logged out by immigration, she was on the plane, there's a record of her arriving in Sydney, the whole nine yards. The police have been round there to tell her the news and made a positive identi –'

'What?' barked Jericho, and his face contorted again at the sudden movement in his neck. He took a moment to allow the shooting pain to die down, a breath, and then said, 'I said I wanted to be the one telling her the news. I needed to be in on that.'

'It was the boss,' said Krause.

'Whose boss?'

'*The* boss,' said Krause. 'The superintendent. She said to not let you tell her. Said you're not great with breaking bad news. Not great with the families.'

'Did she?'

'Yes. And you know, having seen you with Mrs Ravenwood…'

'Thank you, constable. Do we have any news on what her reaction was?'

'She cried a lot.'

'Did she?'

'Apparently. The police said she was very upset. She's already booked to come home, arriving back at Heathrow at 10:25 tomorrow evening from Sydney.'

Jericho nodded, started running his hands together. Felt cold. Needed to go for lunch.

'You think she had an accomplice?' asked Krause.

'I don't know. Let's meet her off the plane tomorrow and start finding out.'

He stood up slowly, trying to straighten his neck, embracing the hurt.

'How about you?' asked Krause, his face contorting slightly in sympathy as he watched Jericho try to straighten his neck out. 'Did you get anywhere?'

'Yes,' said Jericho, now standing still, tensing his shoulders. 'The bookshop was a money pit, but it didn't matter as the deceased had made his millions in the City. He retired out here to be a gentleman bookshop owner in the country.'

'So the widow stands to benefit?'

'Let's see,' said Jericho. 'Maybe Mrs Ravenwood stands to benefit. You can get in touch with the lawyers after lunch.'

'Cool,' said Krause, clicking his fingers. 'Will do.'

Jericho stopped for a second, contemplating further instruction, and then he started walking slowly, as if his legs were hurting as much as his neck, towards the canteen.

'You can still smell that Deep Heat,' said Krause to his back. 'Kinda lingers, eh?'

Jericho hesitated, took a deep breath, and then walked on.

5

Heathrow, Terminal 3, Passport Control. Jericho and Krause were waiting for the passengers from flight EK008 from Dubai. They had ascertained that Rosalind Parks had boarded the flight in Sydney, and had been on board after the stop-off in Dubai. Somehow, and for no reason that Jericho could fathom, he still didn't believe it.

They were standing to the side, looking as obvious as two men in suits invariably look in this situation. They'd spoken to Passport Control, but hadn't come to any particular arrangement, other than that they would pick up Mrs Parks after she'd passed through.

Jericho saw her coming the instant she'd turned the corner away to his left, still seventy yards from the gate. Languid steps, as if she were walking in slow motion. She wasn't beautiful, she wasn't tall, her clothes were not particularly striking, yet somehow she stood out from the crowd.

And there, from that distance, Jericho felt the instant pull of attraction. He lowered his head for a second, managed to stop the heavy and obvious sigh that he could feel coming. It never went well when he wanted to have sex with the suspects/witnesses/family members.

'You all right?' asked Krause.

Jericho lifted his head and nodded in the direction of the widow Parks.

'That's her,' he said.

Krause glanced towards the crowd. Parks had joined the back of a queue, and for Krause at least, she did not stand out.

'Don't see her,' he said. 'Is she in black?'

'She's wearing a lilac pashmina, at the back of the third queue from the left.'

A moment, Krause scanned the crowd, he nodded.

'Got her,' he said.

Jericho remained silent, as the two men watched her, unseen.

'Doesn't look too upset,' said Krause after a while. 'For someone who's just lost her husband to a brutal murder.'

* * *

Jericho did not want to treat the woman who had been in Australia at the time of the crime as a suspect, so they were having coffee at Costa on the ground floor of Terminal 3, just outside arrivals. Two normal people having coffee after a long flight, before hitting the M4. Jericho had dispatched Krause to wait in the car, and was already wondering why it was that he'd brought him along in the first place.

They sipped coffee in brief silence. Jericho could smell her, a delicate, oriental scent. He was glad he'd showered, glad he hadn't felt the need to wear any Deep Heat.

'When was the last time you saw him?' he asked eventually. Had to stop himself staring at her lips, the pink mark they left on her coffee cup.

'Ten days ago,' she said. 'I spent a couple of days in London with my sister before I went to Oz.'

'I thought your sister lived in Sydney?' he said, and was immediately grateful that Krause hadn't been there to hear the stupidity of the question.

'I have more than one sister,' she said coolly.

'Of course.'

She smiled, something wicked about the movement of her lips. He shook himself mentally, tried to detach, tried to get back to treating her like he treated all interviewees.

'You don't seem particularly bothered your husband's dead,' he said bluntly.

She laughed gently, a genuine smile stayed on her lips. He couldn't tell if she was toying with him, or whether this disarming and beautiful display was as real as the smile.

'He was awful,' she said, 'so why would I care? He was a rude, abusive, miserable, miserable man. God knows how he managed to find three mistresses.'

Three mistresses, the number casually thrown into the conversation.

'We got the report that you cried a lot when you heard the news.'

He caught the flash of uncertainty, the hint of discomfort, which was then effortlessly shrugged away.

'It's what's expected of the poor widow, isn't it? I wasn't going to get into discussions about my husband's failings with the local police out there.'

He nodded, looked disinterested.

'Tell me about the mistresses. Because he was rich, presumably, if his character was as objectionable as you say?'

'That would account for two of them. Mrs Ravenwood, on the other hand,' she said, saying the name with a tone which suggested envy, 'seemed to love him for who he was. If you can believe it.'

'Do you have the names of the other two?'

'Of course. Wells is a very small place. Even if we do have the most famous detective on the planet,' she added, her lips curling into the wicked smile again.

'Surprised you came back,' said Jericho glibly. 'Making sure he's dead?'

She smiled again, ran a hand through her hair.

'The good wife,' she said. 'I probably ought to attend the funeral.'

6

Jericho stood looking out of the window of the small terraced house. All he could see was the other side of the street. Krause was looking at that morning's Daily Star. The object of their visit, Margaret Cowan, the next in line of Parks's mistresses, had insisted on making a cup of tea.

'Apparently Alexis is getting her breasts deflated,' said Krause, turning the page.

Jericho stared absent-mindedly out of the window. He was thinking about the murder of Jeffrey Parks, fifty-seven, and the likelihood of it being related to the fact that he'd had four women in his life. Anyone who was sleeping with four women at the same time, thought Jericho, probably deserved to get murdered. He turned eventually, long after Krause had moved on to the next story.

'Who?' he asked.

'What?' said Krause, looking up.

'Am I supposed to know who that is?'

'Who?'

'Alexis?'

'Right. Yeah, Alexis. She's umm… you know, she does stuff.'

Jericho's face was blank.

'She's a model. Huge breasts,' said Krause in response. 'At least, they used to be huge, but now might be a bit smaller. Alexis of Sophie and Gaz.'

'I don't know who Sophie and Gaz are.'

'Sophie's name for when she gets her breasts out is Alexis. She uses Sophie when she writes books and stuff. Although, she doesn't actually write the books, just has her name put on them.' A beat. 'They met on *Love Island*, though they weren't actually a couple on *Love Island*. Everyone was talking about it.'

'Promise me, Constable,' said Jericho, 'that from now on you'll only read grown-up papers.'

Krause smiled. 'If you can find one in the UK, I'll give it a shot, sir.'

Margaret Cowan walked into the room, without the expected tea tray in her hands, and sat down on the sofa opposite Krause.

She sighed heavily and leaned forward, elbows on her knees.

'Tea's off,' she said, looking at Jericho.

There was a pause. Jericho waited.

'I didn't kill him,' she said abruptly. 'But I know who might have.'

Krause laid the paper down and sat forward.

'Oh, for crying out loud,' said Jericho.

'What?'

Jericho took a small notebook from his pocket, scribbled something on a piece of paper, tore the paper out, folded it and handed it to Krause.

'Go on, Mrs Cowan,' said Jericho. 'Who d'you think?'

She looked slightly concerned at Jericho's behaviour, glanced at Krause, and then said, 'Ilsa Ravenwood. That little witch who worked with Jeffrey at the bookshop.'

She stopped talking as Jericho nodded to Krause, and Krause unfolded the piece of paper. The handwriting was hurried and borderline unreadable, yet Krause could still make out the name of Ilsa Ravenwood. He folded the paper back into his pocket, smiling to himself.

'What?' asked Margaret Cowan.

* * *

'How did you know?' asked Krause, as they walked up past Tesco, on their way to the small house near St. Cuthbert's, where they would find the fourth woman in Jeffrey Parks's abruptly terminated life.

'Are you learning?' asked Jericho.

'I'm not learning anything,' said Krause. 'But I'm impressed. What's the secret?'

'The secret, Constable, is paying attention.'

He walked on. Krause followed, unsurprised at the taciturnity.

'You'll find,' said Jericho, after a while, 'our next interviewee also believes Mrs Ravenwood guilty of the murder.'

Krause stopped himself asking how Jericho knew. Maybe, he thought, it would be best if he just paid attention.

* * *

5.30 in the evening of a gloomy Friday. The supermarkets aside, the shops were closing for the night, darkness had already fallen. There were still people abroad on Wells High Street, a majority of them in the uniforms of the Cathedral School or the Blue School, teenagers who didn't care about the rain, who still walked happily in the cold and bleak murk of early evening.

As Jericho and Krause walked back down through the town to the station, bent into the wind and the rain, at the other end of town the blinds had been drawn on the bookshop out on the old Bath Road. Ilsa Ravenwood had, sure enough, been pegged as the murderer by the third of Jeffrey Parks's lovers, Catherine Pitt. It seemed that each one of Parks's women had known about the others, and at least one of them had not been happy about it.

However, as night fell on the city, and the doors were closed and the metal blinds pulled on the shoplife, one thing was certain. The murderous one of the quartet was not Ilsa Ravenwood.

She sat in the same chair behind the counter into which Krause had eased her two days previously. After two days, distraught at the death of her lover, her tears had stopped, to be replaced by the slow drip of blood. The knife had been thrust into her neck from behind, ending her life in a sudden and unexpected moment of searing pain.

The same angle of attack as that which had killed Parks, the same method, the same brand of knife left buried to the hilt in the flesh.

* * *

Jericho and Krause were sitting in his office looking at the whiteboard. There was a photograph of Parks's corpse in the middle, pictures of his four women surrounding it, various arrows drawn between them.

'It doesn't have to be one of the women,' said Krause, after a period of silence. 'The guy was an asshole. There could be a queue of people with a grudge.'

'Yep, but let's not ignore what's in front of our faces. The guy was a horrible man, horrible enough to have quite happily let all his lovers know they were one of a crowd. He made his money legitimately, he sold up his business in a straightforward manner. There are going to be people he pissed off, certainly, but murder… Let's concentrate on what we know, what we've got a feeling for,' and he pointed at the board, his hand moving around the pictures of the four women. 'One of these women,' he added. 'It's about the women.'

'What if there's a fifth woman? One the others didn't know about.'

'Good thought,' said Jericho. 'However, Tom's been all over his computer and his phone. Parks communicated a lot, at least with the three who weren't his wife. It's plausible he didn't tell them about a fifth woman, but seems implausible that he never contacted her. Let's stick to these four for now. Only if we exhaust the obvious, do we progress to the dubious.'

Krause laughed.

'See,' he said. 'That's the kind of snark Sherlock Holmes used to come out with.'

'I'll make sure not to say it again,' muttered Jericho.

There was a brusque knock at the door, which Jericho recognised as that of Constable Tom Patterson, who entered and looked with a raised eyebrow at the graphics on the board.

'You've lost one of your suspects,' he said abruptly.

'Hah!' said Jericho, straightening up. 'Has to be Mrs Ravenwood.'

Patterson nodded, with a glance at Krause. Jericho quickly rose from his chair.

'Let's get over there. Knife in the neck?'

'Knife in the neck,' repeated Patterson.

And off they went, a killer to chase down.

7

The man from the Wells Journal was nosing around outside the shop. A few other gloaters were at the police barriers, hoping for a view of the kill. There were nine police officers at the scene, plus four SOCOs who'd travelled up from Taunton.

Jericho was standing to the side, watching the post-murder investigation unfold. The body had been discovered by Mr Ravenwood, who'd come looking for his wife, late home from work. He was currently sitting in a back room, holding an un-drunk cup of tea, staring at the floor, being attended to by a constable.

Jericho looked sullen, perhaps even bored. However, beneath the surly and aloof exterior, his mind was flying over all the possibilities. The man Ravenwood, while not appearing to be aware that his wife had been romantically involved with Parks, could have taken out his wife and her lover. Perhaps someone had a grudge against the shop in particular, and would now be going after Caroline, the Saturday girl.

Krause appeared from the back room and approached Jericho, hands in pockets. The body was just about to be bagged and removed.

'How's your theory standing up, sir?' asked Krause. 'Do we include the husband in the list of obvious suspects, or do we reduce it to two?'

Jericho gave it a moment, then raised his eyebrow at the latter observation.

'Two?' he said.

'Two girlfriends left. Margaret Cowan and Catherine Pitt.'

'You're ruling out the wife?'

'She was in Australia.'

Jericho stared sceptically at the corpse of Ilsa Ravenwood, as it was manoeuvered into a large, black plastic body bag.

'I'd like you to get hold of Mrs Parks's mobile phone records for the last ten days. No… call it the last month. Let's see if her phone actually went to Australia.'

'You're presuming if the phone didn't, she didn't?'

Jericho turned and gave him a nod of confirmation.

'What about Mr. Ravenwood?'

Jericho turned distractedly back to the corpse, now enveloped in black.

'I'll get Patterson or Collins to look into it. You get on with the phone records. And these sisters of Mrs Parks, do some digging on them as well. I think we need to know a little bit more about them.'

8

Jericho knocked on the door at a little after 8:15pm. Rosalind Parks answered in her pyjamas, with a smile. He looked over her shoulder, expecting to see some other man there for the evening.

'Already in bed?' he asked.

'Curled up on the sofa, eating ice cream, watching a movie,' she said. 'Come in.'

She stood back to let him in, he could smell her as he walked past. She closed the door and led him into the front room. There was a large television in the corner, a film paused mid-frame. On the table were three tubs of ice cream. Triple chocolate, strawberry, and raspberry and vanilla. She lifted the chocolate tub, and settled back onto the sofa, flicking the movie back on as she went.

'Have a seat. Help yourself to ice cream. I've used those spoons, but I don't mind you using them too. We can share.'

He watched the television for a few seconds, then looked at her. There was nowhere else to sit, except beside her on the sofa. The buttons in her pyjamas had parted, and from where he stood he could see the curve of her left breast, the edge of her nipple.

He quickly looked back at the television.

'What are you watching?'

She smiled without looking at him, enjoying his hesitation. Perhaps imagining she was toying with him more than she was.

'An Iranian movie called *Frontier Blues*. It's set on the border with Turkmenistan. I didn't even realise Iran *has* a border with Turkmenistan. It's rather beautiful but not a lot happens. I suppose not a lot happens in real life either. You should sit down.'

'Ilsa Ravenwood is dead,' said Jericho, with his trademark terseness.

Rosalind Parks did not look at him. He watched the flick of her tongue as she licked ice cream from the spoon.

'How tragic,' she said eventually, then she finally turned, her face expressionless. 'On the plus side, that's one less awkward meeting at Jeffrey's funeral. You will come?'

She licked a piece of chocolate from the corner of her lips. Suddenly he stopped finding it alluring, a more familiar annoyance bringing a twitch to the corner of his mouth.

'Where were you three hours ago?'

She studied him while taking another spoonful of ice cream.

'I was here,' she said. 'Alone. Eating ice cream. There are empty pots in the garage if you want to check.'

'And there'll be no one who can confirm that then?'

She shook her head. Continued to eat ice cream in an erotic manner, seemingly unaware she'd lost her audience.

'You'll just have to trust me. Why don't you sit down? Give me an alibi for this evening in case someone else gets murdered.'

Jericho stared at the empty space on the sofa and had one of those moments of self-loathing.

9

The morning was bright. A good day for a murder, if there was to be another one. The previous evening, Jericho had finally left the widow Parks in order to inform the other grief-stricken girlfriends of the latest death. Neither of them had been especially bothered by the demise of Ilsa Ravenwood, just as neither of them had had an alibi. It seemed that none of these women had had much of a life outside of Jeffery Parks. He must have been a busy man, Jericho had thought to himself.

He was sitting at a table in the canteen, scratching his four day old stubble, slowly drinking his third coffee of the day. He looked up as Krause came and sat beside him, armed with a full breakfast and three slices of toast.

'All right?' said Krause, settling down, spearing a sausage before he'd made contact with the seat.

'Yes,' said Jericho. 'Tell me about the widow's phone.'

'Straight down to business, eh?' said Krause.

Jericho didn't reply. He glanced at Krause's breakfast, but was neither tempted nor hungry.

'It checked out,' said Krause through a mouthful of food. 'It had been used in Australia, local calls. The sisters check out, too. One of them was in Sydney with Parks, the other lives in Lee, south of London.'

'Has she got an alibi for the night of Parks's murder?'

'Haven't checked that yet, sir. You think we should cast the net that wide?'

'The net's width is currently infinite, but to be honest, constable, I don't think establishing the widow's sister's whereabouts at the time of the murder is casting the net *at all*.'

'I'll make some calls,' said Krause.

Jericho thought for a moment then shook his head.

'I'm going up to London, I want to speak to her. You can join me if you like.'

Krause continued to shovel food. Finally he swallowed much too big a mouthful without chewing it properly and waved his fork in Jericho's direction.

'I feel you're kind of obsessing about Rosalind Parks, sir. She was in Australia. We *know* she was in Australia. There are several other potential killers out there, there are avenues we're not even exploring, yet we're spending all our time on this one.'

Jericho drained his coffee, laid the cup back in the saucer, and stared at the table for a moment. To his left, Krause crammed in another mouthful of food, and that seemed to be the impetus Jericho needed to move.

'Right at the start,' he said, getting to his feet, 'when you wanted me to say who I thought did it, I was being flippant with my answer. But you know what? I was right. So, you've got ten minutes to eat that lot, then we'll need to go. We should be back around seven, then you can come with me and we'll go and arrest Mrs Parks.'

'Shouldn't we arrest her now, if you're so sure?'

'Don't have enough yet. But we will. Just have to hope she doesn't murder anyone else in the meantime.'

'If you need anything from the sister, shouldn't you just get the locals up in London to go round? I mean, you want to take the entire day out for this?'

A pause. Jericho had been conducting the conversation staring idly across the canteen, out of the high windows at the grey day outside.

Finally he turned and looked at Krause, then said, 'Yes. I do. Sometimes you just have to see people for yourself. Ten minutes.'

Then he turned and walked slowly from the canteen, his shoulders slightly hunched. Krause wondered if Jericho still had a sore neck, or whether he always walked like that anyway, and if the weight of being the country's most successful detective dragged him down.

10

They sat on the train up to Paddington. A little over three hours travelling time in all before they arrived at the house of Rosalind Parks's sister. Krause had tried talking, but almost as soon as the trip began, Jericho had felt the encroachment of depression; his replies had become shorter and shorter.

He had compelled himself to do this, but he didn't want to go back to London. There was too much there. And to Paddington in particular. Where the ghosts were. Where he had last seen Amanda.

He didn't know where she was now. If by some impossible chance she was still alive, she wouldn't be at Paddington Station, yet so much of him was still stuck there, still trapped looking over his shoulder, the last time he saw her. A quick smile, a final glance.

It wasn't supposed to have been the final glance. He hadn't known it at the time. Hadn't even had a strange feeling, an inkling, a premonition. Where had his famous police instinct been that morning?

Sitting uncomfortably on the train, he wondered why he'd invited Krause along. Yes, he himself had to be there. He wanted to meet the sister, to confirm his theory. For all his outward confidence, for all that he projected the image of being in control and knowing everything that was going on, this was just a hunch. He needed to confirm the hunch himself, not rely on Krause.

But why bring him at all? Was it just the instructions from the top, to take the kid under his wing, show him the ropes, before he headed off down to Taunton? Or had he needed the company, the shadow, even though he had no need for conversation? Someone there, beside him, someone to anchor himself to, so that he wouldn't go astray. His mind couldn't travel too far, he couldn't get too lost, because he had a charge. And the charge may not have been a pet or a child or anything or anyone that needed looking after, but it would be just enough to stop him losing contact with reality, drifting uncontrollably into the past.

Nevertheless, at some point he intended that he and Krause

split up, as there was more than one thing to do in the capital, and he just had to hope his head was in the right place when the time came.

* * *

The Tube was packed, every carriage like a rush hour commuter train. They stood in amongst tourists. Krause enjoyed it. The crush of people, the noise, the vibrancy, the adverts on the walls, the great rush of life. Compared to this, Wells was a one-horse town in the middle of nowhere. He would have said so to Jericho, but Jericho had shut down. His eyes were open, but his stare was empty. Krause had heard he had days like this, but he'd yet to see it in the few weeks he'd been at the station. He wondered if he'd have to take over when they got to see the widow's sister.

The train out to Lee wasn't so busy, and by the time they walked out of the station and along the back roads to the semi-detached Edwardian home, the crush of central London was well behind them, a pale winter sun was shining and Jericho was able to emerge slightly from the shell he had constructed around himself.

Nevertheless, when they stood at the door and rang the bell, Jericho had not uttered a word since just after they'd left Pewsey station, over two hours previously.

Janine Miller opened the door and smiled at them both. Black hair was drawn back tightly from her face, just long enough to be tied at the back. She wore thick-rimmed glasses that Jericho thought might be a few years too young for her, and which Krause thought were at least twenty years too young for her.

'Come in,' she said, not bothering to ask for identification. They had arranged their visit.

There was coffee already made, waiting on the table, as if she'd been looking out for them. Hot milk. Three cups. Brown sugar in a small, elegant bowl. No biscuits, no cake. She already knew how Jericho took his coffee. They were all settled in seats, not another word had been spoken, when she said, 'Milk? Sugar?'

'Yes, two sugars please,' said Krause, and he glanced at Jericho. No reply, then the two coffees were handed over and he wondered how Janine Miller had known what Jericho would want.

They each took a sip of coffee and then, like a trio of well-rehearsed synchronized swimmers, laid their cups back on the low table that separated them.

Miller looked expectantly at them, her eyes moving between the two. Krause wondered if he was going to have to say something, and wasn't sure of the line that Jericho had intended taking.

A noise escaped his lips as he started to formulate his first question, but he was immediately cut off by Jericho.

'Did you kill your brother-in-law?'

The voice was flat, matter-of-fact. Krause stared at the carpet, even though he knew he should have been looking at Miller to see her reaction. As it was, there was nothing to see.

'Why would I have done that?' she asked.

Her voice was completely neutral, and yet totally different from thirty seconds earlier. Krause looked up.

'He was a monstrous asshole, and your sister asked you to.'

Miller laughed. She looked curiously at Jericho, wondering if he was being serious, and then a genuine smile started to spread across her face.

'She said you were a piece of work.'

'Did you kill him?'

'No.'

'Your sister came to stay with you before she went to Australia?'

'Yes,' said Miller. 'Just for a couple of nights. We went to see *Warhorse*. I know, but everyone's been talking about it.'

'And you've been here since then?'

'Went to Edinburgh.'

Jericho had been expecting her not to have been there the whole time. He would ask her for proof of her visit to Edinburgh and she would have it, neatly tucked away, train tickets and hotel receipts.

'You can prove that?' he asked.

'Oh,' she said, and she looked over her shoulder, furrowed her brow. 'Yes, I might be able to. You see, I never throw away receipts and what-not until I get the card bill in. I like to crosscheck.' She smiled, looked embarrassed. 'My sisters tell me I'm on the spectrum. You know, Asperger's. I alphabetize absolutely everything, and I can multiply three hundred and twenty-six by nine thousand, three hundred and forty-one in under a second.'

She smiled again, from one of them to the other.

'What is it?' asked Krause.

'Sorry?'

'What is it?'

'What's what?'

'Three hundred and twenty-six times nine thousand, three hundred and forty-one.'

'Oh... seven hundred and ninety-five thousand, two hundred and fifty-six.'

She smiled awkwardly, as if she'd just let them in behind the mask. Jericho took another long drink of coffee, laid the cup back down on the table, stood up and said, 'Thank you very much.'

'Oh,' she said again. 'You don't want to see the receipts?'

'No.'

He looked down at her for a moment, wondering whether it was worthwhile saying anything else, decided that he didn't feel like talking, and walked to the door. Krause glugged the rest of his coffee, put down the cup, rose at the same time as Miller and smiled. Decided that he better not say anything, as his previous contribution was quite possibly already more than Jericho had wanted him to say.

Jericho did not turn. He was not in the mood to be lied to. He opened the door and walked out into the fresh air, the day beginning to cool to a crisp, winter's afternoon. He hadn't noticed it before, even though they'd been in Miller's house less than five minutes.

Krause nodded at Miller and caught up with Jericho as he got to the end of the garden path and turned onto the pavement. She watched them go from the door, not entirely sure what had just happened, waited until they were out of sight and then returned inside to call her sister.

'It's three million, forty-five thousand, one hundred and sixty-six,' said Jericho.

Krause looked at him for a second, then realised what he meant.

'She made up an answer?'

'Yes.'

'She was justifying keeping receipts by trying to establish a condition that she doesn't have.'

'Yes.'

'So she never went to Edinburgh?'

'She never went to Edinburgh.'

'So, she murdered Parks? Why are we leaving?'

'She didn't murder Parks,' said Jericho. 'Her sister murdered Parks.'

Krause nodded. He thought he'd been doing all right.

'I'm experiencing a disconnect,' said Krause.

'You ever see *Duck Soup*?' said Jericho, forcing words he didn't feel like saying.

'What's that?'

'Marx Brothers.'

Krause shook his head.

'I didn't mean you to leave,' said Jericho.

'What?'

'You go back, talk to her. Find out what you can. Get all the information on the trip to Edinburgh she never took. Look at the receipts. The more she says, the more she'll be lying. Probably best not to let her know that you know she's lying. Let her talk, let her hang herself. Make notes… I've got somewhere to go. Meet you back at Paddington in two and a half hours. Don't be late.'

Krause stopped walking. Jericho walked on without looking at him.

* * *

They met again at Paddington, ten minutes behind schedule. They sat and drank another two cups of coffee. Jericho didn't eat anything, Krause had two sandwiches, talking all the while about Janine Miller and what he thought might be relevant. Jericho listened and did not speak. They got on the afternoon train back to the South West and arrived at Castle Cary at 18:45.

11

This time she wasn't wearing pyjamas, but her look was still dressed down and alluring. She welcomed them in, giving Krause an appreciative glance as they passed her in the hall.

'Tea?' she said, having shown them into the front room. An empty tub of ice cream, spoon propped on the edge, sat on the table. The TV was turned off, a couple of magazines lay on the floor.

'Thank you,' said Krause.

'Yes,' said Jericho. 'And cake, if you've got any left, thanks.'

She smiled and left them, walking through to the kitchen. Krause looked curiously at Jericho, having picked up on the vibe.

'If you've got any left? How long did you stay last night?'

Jericho was feeling the relief of being away from London. The pressure had lifted. London compressed him, squeezed him into a black ball. Getting out, sitting on the train heading in the other direction, released him from the oppression. At least for a short time.

'A while,' said Jericho, though not in the least defensively. 'We watched an Iranian movie. Nothing happened in the movie. She offered me ice cream. I don't like ice cream. So she offered me cake. I ate cake. I left. I just asked her if she had any more cake. Are you apprised of the facts, or would you like to know anything further?'

Krause settled into the sofa and lifted a copy of *Town & Country*.

'I'm curious as to whether we're really about to arrest her. Apart from that, I'm pretty cool.'

Jericho grunted, then stood in the middle of the room with his arms folded, staring at the walls.

'Seems a bit off to let her go and make tea, when she's about to be nicked. I don't think they tell you about that in training college.'

Krause looked up at Jericho, who shrugged.

'I'm hungry,' he said.

Krause read an article about foxes. Jericho looked at the walls. Eventually Rosalind Parks returned with the tray. She laid it on a small table, handed the two men a piece of cake each.

'It's yesterday's, but sometimes cake tastes better the next day, doesn't it?'

'We're here to arrest you for the murder of your husband, Mrs Parks,' said Jericho. 'And for the murder of Ilsa Ravenwood early yesterday evening. I must warn you that anything you say will be taken down, and may be used against you in a court of law. Thanks for the cake, by the way. You're right,' he added with a full mouth, 'it is a bit tastier, even if it has lost a certain amount of moisture.'

She looked at Krause, her eyebrow twitching slightly, then back to Jericho.

'You must think I have very long arms, Chief Inspector,' she said.

Jericho nodded, his mouth full of cake.

'If you'd gone to Australia, yes. But since you never got any further than Paris, we can afford to leave the length of your arms out of it.'

Krause was looking at Parks as Jericho spoke, and saw the movement in her face for that brief second. Just an instant, but it was all there. The guilt, the fear, the loathing. Then she flicked the switch and her face returned to showing neutral interest, as if Jericho had just told her she had a problem with her gearbox and her car would need to go into the garage for a couple of days.

'I went to Terminal 3,' said Jericho. 'Had a look at their CCTV. Your sister went to Australia on your passport. You look similar enough, the photo is old enough that she could get away with it, she got her hair done the way you had it nine years ago. Then two days ago you went to Paris on a false passport, just so that you could return at the same time as your sister. You met in the toilets at Heathrow the other side of passport control, swapped passports, you emerged to be met by us at Border Control with your own passport, for all the world as if you'd just been to Sydney. All three sisters in on the lie.'

She breathed heavily, controlling the emotion. Krause was aware that he was sitting there, a bit of a village idiot, no real idea what was going on, looking at the two protagonists in turn with fascination and little understanding.

'She doesn't look anything like her sister,' he found himself saying.

Jericho didn't look at him. He was staring at Parks. She smiled sweetly at Krause.

‘Thank you,’ she said. ‘At least one of you is talking sense.’

‘In the meantime,’ said Jericho, ‘you travelled about a bit, laid the alibis for your sister – which were never going to be watertight, but you just had to hope were enough – and, of course, killed your husband. Having attempted to lay the proof of your innocence for that murder, you then killed Ilsa Ravenwood in exactly the same manner, hoping it would show you also to be innocent of her murder. Sadly, for you, it didn’t.’

Rosalind Parks bent down and lifted a cup of tea. She blew seductively across the top, sucking the men in with her slow movements, giving herself time to think. What they knew and what they didn’t.

‘But I didn’t kill Jeffrey. Why would I do that when there were so many other people queuing up to do it?’

‘There weren’t,’ said Jericho, his words barely understandable, as he’d just taken a mouthful of cake. He chewed, he swallowed, he took some more tea. ‘The others all came in knowing he was married, knowing there was a harem. Only you’d become involved with him expecting monogamy. Only you were actually annoyed by it, while the others just took what they could get.’

‘Maybe,’ she said quickly, ‘but that doesn’t prove anything.’

‘I know.’

There was a pause. She could have laughed, and might have done so had she been someone else. Rosalind Parks was too cool for that, however.

‘So, what evidence do you have for these ridiculous allegation?’

Jericho popped a last piece of cake into his mouth and licked his fingers. Then, keeping his audience waiting, he lifted his cup of tea, cleared his mouth and straightened up. Insomuch as he ever straightened.

‘To be honest,’ he said, ‘that thing I said when I came in, about you being under arrest for the murder blah blah... I just made that up. Wanting to see your reaction.’

Krause glanced at him, even more curious. The Cathedral widow smiled.

‘I’m sorry to leave you so devastatingly empty-handed.’

‘On the contrary,’ said Jericho. ‘Come on, you’re nicked.’

She looked confused, then said, ‘For this absurd passport thing?’ trying to laugh.

‘Sure. Then there’s the fact that you gave your passport to

your sister to travel, then swapped passports. It'll add up. In these days when the border control people are peeing their pants about terrorism, we can get you down for a decent sentence. Meanwhile, we'll go over every single inch of your house and your effects, and at some point we'll nail you. And in the meantime, you won't be able to kill either of these other deluded women.'

He looked down at Krause, who was sitting with his mouth slightly open.

'Finish your cake,' said Jericho. 'We're leaving. Mrs Parks, you're coming into custody. You might want to put a bra on.'

She sneered. 'I'm phoning a lawyer first.'

'Of course you are. Get her to meet you at the station.'

12

Later that evening Jericho was sitting in his office, a solitary sidelight on his desk, looking out on the few lights of the country, stretching out towards the south east. Tenth cup of coffee of the day, which was a lot, even for him. He was aware of Krause walking into the room, and then the constable came and stood beside him, looking out of the window.

'She really doesn't look anything like her sister,' said Krause after a few moments.

'There's usually a similarity with siblings,' said Jericho. 'Much easier for them to pull off the disguise. Watch the mirror scene from *Duck Soup*. Those guys didn't look anything like each other. But watch that scene…'

Duck Soup. Krause had forgotten about that. He could YouTube it when he got back to his office.

'So, is that it?' asked Krause.

Jericho turned and looked at him.

'Pretty much,' he said. 'We'll get her with something. Might take a day or a week or a few months, but we'll get her.'

'What if it wasn't her?'

'And she just pretended to go to Australia, because that's what people do?'

'I suppose.' He paused, thought of something else. 'What about that thing you said a couple of days ago? Never make your mind up until you've got concrete proof?'

Jericho shrugged.

'Did I say that?'

'Yeah. I wrote it down.'

'It goes hand in hand with *always follow your gut instinct.* It's juxtaposition. You'll figure it out in the end.'

A silence settled over them, though it was not destined to last for long.

'I just thought…,' said Krause, then his voice drifted off.

'There'd be more car chases and explosions?' suggested Jericho.

'Closure,' said Krause instead.

'Ah,' said Jericho, nodding. 'I'm afraid this is the real world, son. None of your two-hour detective shows on ITV where everything's neatly wrapped up, it turns out the retired sergeant-major did it and he's led away to a life of imprisonment, confessing as he goes. There's no black, no white. Just great swathes of grey. And too many lawyers.'

Krause sighed heavily, shook his head and looked at his watch.

'I need to get going, if that's OK? We can take it up again tomorrow?'

'Sure,' said Jericho. 'What've you got on?'

'Going into Bristol with some friends. There might be alcohol involved.'

Jericho smiled, nodded, waved a dismissive hand, and Krause turned and walked slowly from his office.

Jericho continued to stare out over the dark of night for another few minutes, then eventually he turned and once more opened the file on Mrs Rosalind Parks. The file was slim, but over the next few weeks he knew it would get much thicker, and there was a fair chance he'd be spending a lot more time with her, playing dangerous games in small rooms.

Cold September, And There's Reason To Believe

1

The players.

Baxter: A dreamer. A character about whom movies are made. A romantic comedy, possibly, though he'd have needed a comedy sidekick for the comedy part of the deal. Certainly not an action movie. Going nowhere; yet where some might see a rut, he just saw life. Most days a repeat of the one before, while his imagination flew in all directions.

Leah: The marine biologist. On earth to have fun, playing her part on a small outcrop in the far west of the continent, bigger picture planet saving penned in for a future date, should there still be a planet left to save.

Edgar: Brusque, coarse, detached, has suffered too many fools.

Grieve: TV personality, we will not scrape much below the surface.

Domino: A seal.

* * *

This day, no different from any other. Baxter rode along the winding track, glancing left to the long beach and the sea. Cold already for September, the wind blowing straight in from the Atlantic meant that the weather was the most changeable thing in his life.

He counted the days. No reason for it – this job wasn't a prison sentence – it was something he couldn't help. *Day One*, he'd thought to himself the first time he'd arrived at the small building at the end of the winding track, by the beach and the rocks. Day One had become Day Two. He'd never lost count.

'You should've been a maths genius,' Leah said to him sometimes. She always laughed when she said it. Other people had said it, but Leah was the only one who spoke with an awareness that you either were or were not a maths genius, there was no choice about it, and that an innate comfort with figures didn't make anyone a maths genius anyway. Some were. Some were not. Leah did not know either way about Baxter.

He came around the side of the long, low white building, parked his bike beside the two others, clipped on the lock, stood for a moment looking out to sea, listening to the sound of the retreating tide on the rocks, straightened his shoulders, then walked in through the side door.

Day One Thousand, Three Hundred and Fifty-Seven.

* * *

'There's news.'

Leah and Edgar were sitting at the table in the kitchen. In the far wall there was a window that looked south, over the rocks, and along to Machir Bay. When the tide was out, you could see the beach. Against the long wall, there was an internal window looking out over the room where they cared for the injured and orphaned seals. This room also contained the large pool, which had a seawater passageway to the enclosed outdoor pool.

'That's exciting,' said Baxter.

His voice did not betray any excitement.

He switched on the kettle, asked the question with raised eyebrows, both Edgar and Leah lifted their mugs to indicate they were good, then he placed the teabag in the cup and turned to face them.

Leah, twenty-six, short dark hair, laughed often, lips that Baxter had kissed a thousand times, if daydreaming was the same as doing.

Edgar, weather beaten, grey hair thinning, an old man and the sea. Though still in his early sixties, so perhaps not so old by the standards of the day.

'We've been given a grant by the government, and now we're all going on a fact-finding mission to Iceland?'

'That'd be nice,' said Leah.

'Not yet, but this might help us,' said Edgar.

The kettle rumbled, having boiled not five minutes previously.

'You know Joshua Grieve?'

Baxter stared blankly at them. Leah was smiling.

'The TV travel guy?' she said, nudging.

Baxter looked at her while he searched for the memory of him. He didn't watch TV travel shows anymore. Not since they'd been infiltrated by celebrities. He'd enjoyed Palin at first, but now blamed him.

'I'm not sure I know Joshua Grieve,' he said.

Leah rolled her eyes, but there was an affection in it. *Classic*

Baxter, she might just have thought to herself.

'He does exotic travel shows,' she said. '*Josh's Journeys*. He did Russia, and Australia. He did the length of the Americas last year, he did West Africa. Super interesting.'

'And now, what? He's doing Islay?'

'Yes! Isn't it cool?'

Baxter had no idea about Joshua Grieve, but it seemed incongruous for such a world traveller to be coming to the western isles.

'The producers sent an e-mail. I talked to them last night,' said Edgar. 'He's doing a trip round the coast of Britain, and he's…'

'Didn't someone do that already?'

Leah rolled her eyes again.

'You know what they're like,' said Edgar. 'They make the same shows every three years. Now, it's our turn. The man, this Grieve, is a whisky drinker. Wanted to come to Islay, but they didn't want to just show the man flat out on his arse, hammered.' Leah laughed. 'They asked if we had any seals we might be about to release back into the wild. He'll come here for the day, see what we do…'

'Meet the seals…'

'And with Domino ready to go back, I thought… you know, it might work out well, and the exposure won't do us any harm.'

'What day are we talking?'

'Next Monday.'

Baxter stood and stared. Monday flashed up before him in newspaper headlines. *Day Ruined As TV Crew Butts In. TV Invasion Seals Baxter's Fate. Drunk Travel Celeb Steals Girl.*

The kettle clicked off behind him.

'Cool,' he said, and he turned to pour the water into his mug.

2

Domino was resting by the side of the pool, staring up at Baxter. He was sitting on a seat, the mop in between his legs, looking down at her large, mournful, dark eyes.

The following day. Yesterday's news had become part of the fabric of the sanctuary. It was Baxter's job to keep everything in order, and that part of his personality that made him good with figures and awkward with people, also – in what Leah jokingly called a 'crushing cliché' – made him meticulous and neat, and so there were few preparations to be made for the arrival of the television crew. The seal sanctuary operated in a state of being permanently ready for television exposure, even if none of them had ever previously thought about it.

The night before, Baxter had watched twenty minutes of *Josh's Journeys* on iPlayer. Grieve was young, handsome and funny, and of his time. The walk through the Brazilian rainforest wasn't about the Brazilian rainforest, it was about Grieve walking through the Brazilian rainforest.

'He's good, I'll give him that,' he said.

Domino stared silently back at him. She liked the sound of his voice. In the background, Sinatra was singing. *The Night We Called It A Day*, from one of his late fifties albums; end of the evening, melancholic, the hopeless reverie of lost love.

'Look, you can't complain, can you? The producers, the TV people, they make the shows people want to see, right?'

Domino didn't have a comment on shows, but she recognised Baxter's unhappiness. She flapped one of her flippers on the ground a couple of times, moving slightly nearer towards him. Baxter nodded in return, they held the look for a few moments, and then they both turned towards the pool, the splash on the surface as another of the seals bobbed up. A young female named Tilly.

She looked at them both for a moment, and then ducked her head, swam towards them, waddled up onto the side of the pool, and flopped down beside Domino.

Baxter watched them for a moment then, voice dry and phlegmatic, 'What do I know about shows? I never watch shows.' A beat. 'That, and my best friend is a seal.'

Tilly barked, Domino lifted her head.

* * *

When Domino had arrived at the sanctuary, she'd had a deep laceration on her right side, her tail was badly entangled in industrial fishing wire, and both of her flippers had been damaged. Her recovery had been long and slow. When they would finally set her free, she'd have been with them longer than any other seal bar Honey.

They all remembered Honey, they all remembered the sadness of the day she left. The final look, her head ducking beneath the water, the last glimpse of her tail.

Like all the seals they'd released, Honey had had a tracking device attached to her right flipper. Many of the seals stayed in the area, many of them returned for a visit. Honey, however, had gone. Currently in the northern isles, in the area of Westray. They wouldn't see Honey again.

Baxter's memory of Honey leaving had a completely different focus, however. His memory of the day was about Leah.

It had been one of those moments, so rare in these couple of years. An opportunity that hung in the air, suspended for an infinite few seconds, before it vanished in an indefinable moment.

Honey had gone, Leah had cried, and she and Baxter had found themselves hugging, as unexpected as it had been natural. The feel of her, the smell of her hair! They had leaned back a little, still in each other's arms, the tears on Leah's cheeks, and smiled.

That was the moment. In her eyes as much as his. He could have kissed her. He could have hugged her close again. He felt his self-defence slip away, the years of reserve, hour upon hour of awkward silence, so many words unsaid, a snap of the fingers and they'd be gone, and on the cusp of it – looking back, he was sure he'd been on the cusp of it – 'Come on you two!' came the cry from Edgar, still looking out to sea, and he turned just as Leah and Baxter pulled apart, that shy smile on her lips as the moment was taken from them.

He remembered the look on Edgar's face, though he didn't understand it. Was it regret or disappointment? And what of Leah's eyes, the depths of them as they fell, then she'd turned away and that was it for that particular moment in their lives.

There had been other times he could have said something. Every day he could have *said* something. He never said anything. Leah's boyfriends came and went, every one a potential crushing blow, though they never seemed to stick.

Perhaps he was no longer crushed. Perhaps, now, he had given up, and Leah had become something other than the woman whose smile illuminated his day. She was his lost love, the one who would never be, his excuse to never have to trouble himself with anyone else. He would always have Leah, even if he would never have Leah.

Yet he wondered about the next moment. The departure of the next Honey. When another of their rogue little band of hurt and abandoned seals, who would come under their care, and who would get under their skin, would be set free. And then, when this animal swam off out into the oceans of the world, he and Leah would each be consumed by the same feeling of sadness and celebration, and they would turn to each other, and the hug would be automatic, and this time…

And here was Domino, and Domino had become the next Honey, and soon Domino would be leaving, and for weeks, weeks and months, Baxter had been thinking about it, and trying not to think about it because *you can't overthink spontaneity!* but that moment would come again, and maybe this time it would spontaneously go further than it went the last time.

And it was the measure of him, and his indecision and his lack of confidence, that he'd invested such hope in the moment, rather than investing hope in any other day, when every other day offered an opportunity of being alone with Leah.

He hated the banality of it. How many had been here before? Hopelessly in love, unwilling to make the move for fear of losing what was already there?

And now it was upon them, the time of planned spontaneity, yet from the shadows darkness had sprung, and the light of opportunity would be eclipsed.

* * *

He sat and ate dinner in the small bay window in his kitchen, looking out over the fields that ran down to the rocky shoreline. A glass of pinot grigio, a cod fillet in breadcrumbs, a view of the far horizon.

He didn't watch TV shows, he didn't follow sport. He read books, he listened to Sinatra, and he sat at the window and watched the world come and go. Everything that happened out there, as the awfulness of humanity enveloped the world, happened beyond his horizon. He watched the sea on the rocks, occasionally a boat in the far distance, the clouds as they blew across the sky. On weekends he would ride his bike, go walking in the hills, sometimes go into Bowmore, sometimes take the boat across to Jura. A life of one foot in front of the other, rarely looking beyond the next step, preserving himself with scraps of hope.

That night the scrap of hope was gone, dinner was long and dull, the glass of wine, which became a second and a third, did not help, and Sinatra was not alone in his melancholy.

3

Monday morning. Day One Thousand, Three Hundred and Sixty. Worst fears realised. Joshua Grieve arrived, his crew the vanguard. Producer, two camera operators, a sound engineer, the production assistant. Beth, Maisy, Wyatt, Rose and Brandon. There would be nine people in all to witness Domino's departure.

Grieve was laughing. White teeth. Straight.

'You name all the seals after Bond girls and Bond villains?' he said to Edgar. 'Oh my God, that's the funniest thing I've ever heard!'

'We've got to get that on camera,' said Beth, the producer.

Edgar was not a natural for television. He shrugged, not thinking it all that remarkable. He did not look any happier about the arrival of the crew than Baxter.

'It's so funny,' said Leah.

'I know, right?' said Grieve. He smiled at Leah, looked out over the outdoor pool, to the seals that were currently lying up on the rocks, then turned back to her with a wicked smile.

Here is comes, thought Baxter. *Where's Pussy?*

'Where's Pussy?' said Grieve, affecting a poor Sean Connery, laughing after the joke. Leah laughed with him.

'Gone, I'm afraid,' she said. 'Currently in Iceland.'

'Of course she is,' said Grieve, still with the Connery, then he turned to Beth and said, 'I can do the Pussy gag to camera, right?'

'Sure,' said Beth, 'may as well get the clip. Might not make it to screen.'

'Cool cool,' said Grieve, then he turned back to Leah, lightly touching her arm. 'Maybe you could talk us through all the different seals you have here, not just Domino, and we can get a feel for the whole Bond thing. I love that.'

He turned away from the others, Leah went with him, their backs now to Edgar and Baxter.

Edgar had already told Leah he was looking for her to be the face of the organisation. She was going to look good on camera, he was happy for her to have the limelight.

The producer walked with Leah and Grieve, the rest of the

crew were looking around, taking in the view along the rocky coast, perhaps thinking about light and camera angles, perhaps wondering when they would be offered coffee and bagels.

Baxter watched Leah's back for a moment, then when he forced himself to look away, he noticed Edgar was also watching Leah walk away with Grieve. A look in his eyes that Baxter recognised, then Edgar's gaze dropped, his head dipping slightly with it.

I am not alone, thought Baxter. And there was jealousy, and there was wonder.

* * *

They were sitting on the plastic chairs by the indoor pool. Baxter and Edgar, three seals and two cups of tea for company. Outside the crew had set up, and Leah and Grieve were doing a piece to camera. Baxter had found himself unable to watch. Armed with his new knowledge, he was not surprised to find Edgar had made the same decision to retreat inside.

Sinatra was singing, doleful and low, *Blues In The Night*, while Titania, Aki and Nick Nack lay in a small heap by the side of the pool. The pool was busy, all the other seals currently inside, as the outdoor pool would soon be opened up to the sea to allow Domino to leave.

'It'll pass,' said Edgar into the silence of Sinatra, words appearing in the room from nowhere. 'This blasted whirlwind.'

He didn't look at Baxter as he spoke. He had sounded distant enough that he wasn't speaking to Baxter in any case. The words expressed to himself, perhaps. Baxter had nothing to say to it.

'Though Domino will still be gone,' continued Edgar. A beat. Quiet seconds filled with the blues of a late night bar in the city. 'She's been a good girl.'

How many ways were there to describe silence? This was one of them. One of the silences. Edgar stared at the seals, Baxter stared vaguely at the water, wondering whether Edgar had really been talking about Domino, and he pictured the film crew driving off in their top-of-the-range minibus, Leah now part of the team, waving goodbye as she went.

'What age are you?' asked Edgar, the sounds of language materialising suddenly.

Enveloped in the gloom of the moment, the idea that the woman he loved was slipping away, the words had to penetrate his thick outer shell before getting through.

'Twenty-seven?' said Baxter a few moments later, questioning not whether that was indeed his age, but why Edgar had thought to ask.

'Why are you listening to this? I mean,' and Edgar broke off for a moment, nodding in the direction of the music, before continuing, 'your man's been singing the same fucking song over and over again for the last hour and twenty minutes.'

Baxter laughed, didn't have an answer.

'Every day you listen to this crap. Every day, the same song. You have the same song on repeat, right?'

'You know I don't,' said Baxter.

'Is this a suicide album? Sinatra didn't commit suicide, did he?'

'No!' said Baxter. 'It was just, you know… just market forces, like everything else.'

'Go on.'

Baxter gave Edgar a curious look to see if he was really interested, and got the go-ahead with a small, encouraging nod.

It made sense. Talk about anything other that what was waiting to be talked about; the woman outside, being whisked away from them as they sat there.

'When he started making albums in the fifties for Capitol he liked to give them a theme. Kind of concept albums. And he did one called *In The Wee Small Hours* – people called it the Ava album 'cause he'd split up with Ava Gardner and was miserable – and the album was bluesy and sad and kind of, you know, sitting in a bar at eleven pm with a glass of Bunnahabhain feeling depressed, and people loved it…'

'I bet they did.'

'So he did some more like that. There are a few of them.'

'Which one's this?'

'*Frank Sinatra Sings For Only The Lonely*.'

Edgar laughed at the name.

'This one's about not getting to shag Ava Gardner 'n' all?'

'I don't know,' said Baxter. 'Maybe he was just meeting market demand by this point.'

The smiles died away, another of the silences crept in. The silence became total for a moment, the gap between songs, and then the plucked guitar of *Guess I'll Hang My Tears Out To Dry* began.

They listened for a few moments, and then, as the strings

swept in and sent the song spiralling into the pit of pathos, Edgar shook his head, said, 'Jesus, son,' downed his tea, and got positively to his feet.

'Come on,' he said, 'this isn't helping either of us. We should go out and watch the show, see if Leah needs rescuing.'

He turned away, took another drink from the mug, though only the dregs remained, and then walked through into the next room, leaving the door open. Baxter did not immediately follow, for a moment holding a stare with Aki's doleful eyes, and then Edgar shouted, 'Shift your arse, son!' from the other room.

4

Leah did not look as though she needed rescuing. She and Grieve were kneeling down beside Domino, who was on the rocks by the side of the pool. One of the cameras was filming them, the other was filming the entire scene, including the first camera and the sound engineer. Beth was standing back, watching from a few yards away, although at that moment she was looking at her phone.

When Baxter and Edgar emerged from the building, Brandon, the assistant, who was standing the furthest at the back, pulled what was supposed to be a comedy panicked face, then put his finger to his lips. The men exchanged a glance, as Baxter softly closed the door, and then they walked up beside Brandon.

A moment, then Brandon said, 'They're killing it this take,' in a really low voice. 'It'll be a keeper.'

'You have such an amazing connection with Domino,' said Grieve, as Baxter allowed himself to tune in, filtering out the wind and the sea and the horror of it. 'I travel all over, see all sorts of extraordinary things, but this is something else. It's like… I mean, it's like you really understand each other. Like you can talk to one other.'

'I know what you mean,' said Leah, smiling.

Baxter recognised her discomfort. Or maybe he just hoped it was discomfort. Maybe he was just projecting his own discomfort.

'This must be really tough for you,' said Grieve, 'preparing to let Domino go. So tough…'

Leah had nothing to say. She looked at Domino and then at Grieve. Something about her that said she might be about to cry. The microphone picked up the sound of her swallowing. She *was* about to cry.

Grieve nodded his understanding, unusually recognising it was a moment to stay silent, and then inevitably, horribly, as the wind blew and the sea touched the shore, he reached out to take hold of Leah's fingers. They leaned in towards one another, the first tears appeared on Leah's face, and then they leaned even closer, his arm around her shoulder, their foreheads pressed together.

Grieve's back was turned to them, so they couldn't see if the TV star had managed to conjure his own tears to make the moment even more magical.

Baxter swallowed, though he didn't feel like crying. He glanced at Edgar, who was looking lost. It felt like looking in the mirror.

He turned back to the emotional TV moment, like so many other emotional TV moments, be they about the loss of a partner, or a doomed relationship, a pet's illness or a complete failure of rough puff pastry.

There was a movement behind the weeping TV players, then Domino moved into Baxter's line of vision. The smooth grey head, the sad eyes. She looked at him, she glanced sideways to the sad couple making the moment about them, rather than about her, then she looked back at Baxter.

She smiled.

Not the toothy, goofy grin that seals sometimes pull, the facial expression that humans might anthropomorphise into a smile. This was a genuine smile, as much in the eyes as the slight drawing back of the mouth. She nodded, a final look, eyes that seemed to speak, then she turned away and slid silently into the water.

Leah and Grieve did not notice her departure.

'I can't watch this anymore,' muttered Edgar, and he turned away, ignored the imploring look from Brandon, walked back into the building and slammed the door behind him.

* * *

An hour later. It was time.

A last look, the head poked above the surface of the water, Domino hovered, she held Baxter one last time with her doleful yet hopeful eyes, then she ducked beneath the meagre waves of the outdoor pool, swam towards the gap in the cage, and then she was out into the open sea, and quickly lost in the darkness of the water.

The four of them watched her go, one to four in a line. Grieve, Leah, Baxter and Edgar, filmed from either side, the boom microphone held high above them.

None of them had any words, until Grieve felt the need to provide one.

‘Wow,’ he said.

A moment. No one spoke, the emptiness not allowing the formation of any further words, until Grieve found some more.

‘I think that’s, like, the most emotional thing I’ve ever seen. Just… wow.’

He held Leah’s hand. The camera caught their fingers entwining. She leaned in towards him, resting her head against his shoulder.

5

Seven-fifteen, the bar in the Port Charlotte Hotel. They were sitting at the window in the dining area, looking out at the end of the day on Loch Indaal. Flat calm, high cirrus, tinged with orange. Baxter and Edgar, eating in silence.

The crew were dining in Port Ellen. They'd asked all three of the sanctuary staff to accompany them, only Leah had gone along. She'd tried to get Baxter to join them, and in the end he'd lied and said he was feeling sick.

She had made no effort to get Edgar to accompany them, happy, it seemed, to leave him behind. Baxter was curious, somehow hurt in his exclusion from this drama, of which he had previously been unaware.

They ate the usual food. The evening demanded the tedium of familiarity. Battered fish, thick-cut chips, peas, a pint of cider.

The night before had been jumping in the bar, a folk trio playing. Monday was dead, as though everyone who was going to go to the pub had been the previous evening, and no one could go two nights running. Holiday season was over, the tourists had drifted away, autumn was here, winter was coming.

'What's with you and Leah?' asked Baxter.

He blinked, surprised the words had found their way out into the silence. He'd thought them, certainly, but he had made no positive decision to actually say them out loud. He wasn't sure he even wanted an answer.

Edgar was studiously looking at his fish, as he had been doing since the plate had been placed in front of him. There was a yacht motoring along the centre of the loch, two fishermen on the shore, a beautiful liquidity to the light of the end of the day, but he had given it no time.

He lifted his glass, took a long drink, did not look at Baxter.

'You don't want to talk about that, son,' he said.

'Why did you say to Leah she should be the lead for TV?'

Edgar grunted through his food, a small piece of fish appeared at the side of his mouth. He wiped his lips with the back of hand, looked at the white scrap that had appeared there. Thought about it, and then put his hand to his mouth and ate the fish.

'She asked,' he said gruffly.

'Didn't *you* want to do it?'

'We've met?' questioned Edgar. 'You and me, we've met, right? You know who I am?'

'So, why let them come at all?'

Edgar shook his head, annoyed they were even talking.

'Look at us,' he said. 'Look at us, at our facilities. How small we are, how insignificant, how little good we can actually do. You know we need all the publicity we can get. This guy, this Grieve, he's on BBC1, nine o'clock. People watch that garbage. *They watch it,*' he added, as though it needed emphasising. 'We cannot buy that publicity. I knew as soon as the e-mail came in we'd have to take it, and I can't…'

Another ugly shake of the head, and he stabbed two chips and thrust them into his mouth, like he was eating the flesh of his enemies.

'What?'

Baxter hadn't taken a bite, nor looked out upon the tranquillity of evening, since they'd started talking.

'What can't you do?'

'I can't not take this kind of opportunity because you're going to be upset your girlfriend'll drop her pants the second a good looking TV star comes along.'

Baxter let the words *she's not my girlfriend* lie where they belonged. Now he was left with the conversational hole he'd dug for himself, and the image of Leah and Grieve in bed. Later tonight, or already, right now, back at his hotel room. Leah naked, breathing heavily, on top, his hands, his lips, his tongue all over her.

'You didn't seem so happy about it either,' he said, forcing the conversation deeper into the pit.

'Didn't I?'

'No,' said Baxter. 'When I looked at you, it was like looking in the mirror.'

Edgar grunted again, forced fish into his mouth, took a drink, wiped the rim of the glass. An unhappy silence had been fine for Edgar. Baxter, however, recognised that a great unravelling was taking place. It had begun, and ending it now would leave them uncomfortably suspended in dark half-truths and shades of grey.

'It was like looking in the mirror,' he repeated.

'Was it?'

'Yes. So, what was that? What's between you and Leah?'

'What did you think, son? Hmm? You thought the sun would always shine, and one day Leah would suddenly wake up, decide she loved you, and the two of you would happily go off and have boring little babies together?'

The hurt immediately showed on Baxter's face, and Edgar muttered, 'Fuck,' shook his head again, and held up his knife in apology.

'Sorry,' he said. 'That's... I didn't mean it.' He lowered his head, looked at what was left of his dinner, as he'd been angrily racing through it, the annoyance now dissipating. 'About the babies,' he added, wanting to make the distinction. 'I didn't mean you'd have boring babies.'

'We're not going to have...' began Baxter, then he shook the words away. Pointless words, just as Edgar's had been pointless.

A short gaze across the table, Edgar suddenly looking more sympathetic, then he said, 'You need to move on, son.'

A rueful gesture from Baxter, then, 'I can't... can't get her out of my head. That's how it is. I may have given up, I may have... I don't know, I don't even fantasise anymore, I just drown myself in wine and miserable Sinatra songs. It's just been that way so long, I don't know anything else anymore.'

'You're twenty-seven!' said Edgar, and from nowhere he smiled.

'I know,' said Baxter. 'But... that's all. It's been the better part of three years. Quite long enough to become entrenched.'

Edgar held his gaze across the table, his eyes softening, and then he turned away and looked out across the loch to the lights of Bowmore, away to their left.

'I'm sorry, son,' he said.

'What for?'

Baxter got a sense of it. What was to come. He swallowed. *God, the stupid obviousness of it.*

It hadn't been looking in the mirror at all. That had been more projection on his part. He hopelessly loved Leah, so he assumed Edgar hopelessly loved Leah.

'I've been sleeping with her for a couple of years, son,' said Edgar. 'It's just the way it is. One of those things.'

He brought his eyes back from the water, and stared across the table. The old, rugged face, grey eyebrows, skin weathered by the wind and the sea, grey hair thinning, teeth pale and crooked, the larger than average nose of the drinker in his early sixties, the permanent spiky bristle of five days' beard growth.

‘She was never going anywhere near you, son. You wore it too plainly, your unrequited love. Sleep with you, and she’d have been entangled. All she got from me was sex, which was all she wanted.’ A beat, the tone of his words an acknowledgement he knew how much they’d hurt. ‘And fool that I am, I allowed myself to fall in love with her too. What a clown, right? She’s twenty-six and gorgeous, and I’m a leathery old cunt with about one thing going for me.’

Another beat. Baxter had nothing to say. He’d dug the whole, and now he was lying in the bottom of it, the spade he’d used for digging being used to pound him over the head.

‘We were the same, you and me,’ said Edgar, ‘even if you didn’t realise it. At least I got sex out of it. You just got your shitty Sinatra albums.’

Another moment, finally it seemed that Edgar had finished, the brief flurry of blows was at an end, and he stabbed another couple of chips, jabbed them in ketchup, and forced them into his mouth.

‘Food’s getting cold,’ he said through the chips, ‘you should eat.’

6

Baxter sat on at the window of the bar, looking out on the loch as darkness came, long after Edgar had excused himself with the words, 'Enough of this shit. I'm going home to get drunk.'

The thought of going home was unpalatable to Baxter. Sitting at this window here, a different view on the world, the noise of the bar behind him, quiet though it was, was bearable. Just enough life to be distracting. At home, sitting on his own at his usual window, looking out on the night, listening to Frank, would be wallowing in sorrow.

Would he ever listen to Sinatra again? Those tunes, the sound of that voice, was so entwined with the idea of Leah. The hopeless romance of it. The woman who was there every day, who smiled, who affectionately rolled her eyes, who touched his arm and laughed, and who he would never hold.

He looked across the loch, the rest of the island beyond. The last of the sun was still touching the tops of the hills in the distance, a final moment of colour, and then, as he watched, it vanished. The sun, somewhere far out to the west and out of sight, dipped below the horizon, the hills to the east turned grey in the last of the day's light.

There goes the sun, he thought. There goes Leah.

'No, that's not right,' he said to no one, his voice low against the muted talk from the bar. 'Leah was never with me in the first place. There goes the dream, that's all.'

He shook his head, then added, 'The sun's a fucking metaphor,' then smiled at himself for the profanity. That's what spending time with Edgar did for him.

'Is everything all right for you?'

Snapped from it, he turned quickly. The waitress was standing by his table, a round, brown tray of empty glasses in her hand.

'Yep,' he said quickly, covering the slight awkwardness of being caught talking to himself.

'Would you like dessert?'

'I'm all right, thanks.'

'Are you sure? There's cheesecake!'

She was young, early twenties maybe, and there was a

lightness and attractiveness about her and the tone of her voice, a lightness that was at odds with the forced gloom that had lingered over the table since Edgar had angrily worried his way through dinner.

'What kind of cheesecake?' was all Baxter could think to say.

'Blueberry. It's lovely. I just had a piece,' she said, and she touched the corner of her mouth as she said it, as though she might still have the crumbs on her lips.

'Sure,' said Baxter, 'sounds like a good idea. Blueberry cheesecake it is.'

'Coffee?'

'Just the cheesecake.'

'Good choice!'

She smiled and was gone. Baxter watched her for a second, and then turned back to the view. The grey water, the lights on the opposite shore, the grey hills beyond, the darkening sky.

It was as though the waitress had left something of herself behind. The air was lighter.

He glanced over his shoulder to see if there was any sign of her, and then returned to the view. Didn't take much sometimes, yet the situation remained the same. Over the hill and round the headland, Leah would still be spending the night with Joshua Grieve, and if her return to work in the morning was uncomfortable, it wouldn't be Baxter who'd be the problem.

He lifted his glass of water, unthinkingly, found it empty, poured some more from the small jug, took another drink.

Was it just the magical lightness, left by the waitress, deposited by fairy dust, that was making him feel better, or was the fairy dust bringing out something else within him, the way a little salt draws out the sweetness?

Could that other feeling he was aware of, the one lurking just out of sight, be relief?

Leah didn't love him. (He'd known that all along.) She was never going to love him. (He'd known that too.) When she'd wanted a casual sexual relationship, she'd specifically gone to old Edgar rather than him because there was, she'd thought, less chance of emotional involvement. And now she'd surprised no one by happily going off with the TV personality.

That's who she was. And why shouldn't she be? She was twenty-six years old and beholden to no one.

There may have been no place for logic in love, but why shouldn't he feel relief? The burden of obsession was gone. The thing that had been taken away, was something he'd known he would never have. This wasn't finding out that his girlfriend or wife had been having an affair, this was the cold water being poured on the last meagre flame of hope, and a flame at that which had already burned away to insignificance.

So, why not relief? Wouldn't it make sense, in amongst the hurt? It would be painful, but it could also signal an end to the long, uncomfortable agony. Instead of a gut punch, there could be a lifting of the weight. Instead of horror, there could be emancipation.

'Can I get you anything else?'

Baxter turned to the waitress, an older woman, probably his mother's age, a smile on her face, an empty tray under her arm. Just as he turned, a strand of hair fell across her face, and she blew it away, her bottom lip protruding to direct the air.

'I already ordered cheesecake from the other girl,' said Baxter, 'thanks.'

The waitress looked curious, glanced over her shoulder.

'It's only me.'

'No, there was another girl. Young.'

'It's really only me. I served you the fish supper, remember?'

'Yes, but…'

He held her look for a few moments, then glanced past her, wondering if the girl would be sitting at a table, smiling. Would've been a peculiar practical joke to have played.

'So a waitress appeared out of nowhere, then vanished again?'

'I don't know, there's always a little magic in the air around here. Cheesecake?'

'I guess,' said Baxter.

They were still looking curiously at each other, both a little confused, then the waitress broke the moment, said, 'Cheesecake coming right up!' smiled, and turned away.

Baxter watched her until she'd walked around the side of the bar, and was gone. He looked at the few customers he could see, and then turned back.

He took a drink of water, drained the glass, and placed it back on the table. The lightness, wherever it had come from, remained.

7

The wind was cold in his face, as he rode his bike back up over the hill, and across this side of the island, back down to Machir Bay.

Downhill now, towards the coastline, the light on his bike illuminating the single track road. Beyond the thin beam of light the white forms of huddled sheep were evident in the surrounding fields.

He wasn't sure what was taking him back to the sanctuary. Maybe there was just nowhere else to go. He didn't want to sit drinking in the bar, and while he may have decided he'd be able to embrace relief instead of desolation – still early days to know which way that would go – he knew he didn't want to go home and spend the remainder of the evening, brothers in melancholy with his old Sinatra records.

The sanctuary seemed a sensible place. He liked the quiet of it at night, and even though Domino was gone, the other seals would be happy enough to see him, even if it was only because they thought he might supply them with food.

On a shallow long straight stretch of road, he sat up, stretched his back, rubbed both hands across his face.

The bike wobbled, and he quickly leaned forward again, took hold of the handlebars, automatically applied a little brake. Shook his head at his own chutzpah, slowed some more.

Idiot Falls Off Bike, Replaces Emotional Hurt With Broken Limbs, Crushed Skull.

* * *

He entered the darkness of the office, then turned on the small desk light, and stood for a moment in the quiet of evening. Pitch dark outside, but only just after ten o'clock.

He didn't often come here at night. He had no reason to, not unless one of the seals was ill or needing round-the-clock care. Even then, it was Edgar who was the trained vet, Leah the marine biologist. Baxter was the caretaker, the hired help, the one who made things tick over.

He felt the sadness of it, of course, the sadness of any empty building after dark. There may only have been three of them who worked there, and there were never more than seven or eight seals, but during the day music played, and the place bustled, and all three of them were busy, and the seals came and went, and they played and they barked and they honked, they grunted and they groaned.

Now, at just before ten, the place was asleep. The last time he'd come in at this time, he'd gone and sat by the pool and chatted to Domino. She'd lain down, rested her head on his foot, and looked up at him with those dark eyes, so that he'd felt she understood every word.

He felt it now even more, the haunting emptiness of the night.

Through into the kitchen, the table and the tea point, the room tidied up and sorted after the unusual influx of visitors that day. Without turning on a light, he put some water in the kettle and switched it on. Then he walked to the window, looking into the pool area to see if there were any seals resting at the side of the water.

There was a woman sitting in one of the chairs, bent over, her head in her hands. Dark hair, dank and wet, hanging down over her arms. Naked.

The shock of it, heart and stomach in the mouth, the small ejaculation of sound, and Baxter stood staring into the half-light of the other room, this strange figure in the shadows.

From behind the glass he could see she was shivering. He quickly opened the door, walked through. There were no other seals present, which was not necessarily surprising. They could all still be outside on the rocks.

'Hello?'

He felt no threat. Not that he would have thought, had he thought about it, that he had an innate sense of these things, but nevertheless, this woman would do him no harm.

'Are you all right?' he asked.

She lowered her hands, looking round at him. Even in this strange light he could see she was blue with the cold.

'Sorry,' he suddenly said, and he quickly took off the thick woollen jumper he'd worn while cycling back over the hill and held it towards her.

Nothing.

He took a step closer.

'Go on,' he said. 'You're freezing.'

A moment, and then she reached out to take the jumper. As she did so he caught sight of her naked breast, and turned his head away as she took the clothing from his hand.

Their fingers touched.

He recognised that feeling from his imagination.

* * *

They were sitting at the table. The light was on, cup of tea each, he'd found her a pair of trousers, and a towel for her hair, and he'd set the small convection heater going.

The colour was coming back into her face, she'd stopped trembling. Hands clutched around the warm mug, she was looking at Baxter. Somehow not staring, yet watching closely. She had yet to talk, and Baxter had silently gone about the business of warming her up. He was nervous for a while, but he had caught her eye a couple of times and the look had relaxed him.

I mean you no harm, he imagined her saying, as though she was a visitor from another planet.

'You can put the music on,' she said suddenly. Her voice was soft, a beautiful tone, a lilt from the islands. 'I like it.'

Baxter had just sat down opposite her, and then he stood again, walked over to the small CD player and started off the disc that had been playing that afternoon, *Sinatra Sings Only For The Lonely*, and *Only The Lonely* began, the sound so familiar, as warm as the tea they held in their hands.

He sat down, they stared at each other from across the table. From three feet away, in the warmth of pale light, she was the most beautiful woman, the most beautiful anything, he'd ever seen in his life.

'You're a selkie,' he said, finding the words.

She held his gaze, she let the music play for a while, Sinatra's voice wove in and around them, and eventually she nodded, the mug in front of her face, steam rising across her eyes.

'That's…' he said, but then he let the words go. What was it, exactly? Unbelievable? *You'll need to do better than that!*

'My skin is in the far corner, at the back of the pool. You'll need to hide it, and never tell me where it is.'

'I don't want to trap you.'

'I want to be trapped, if trapped is what you'd call it,' she said. 'And if my skin is out of sight, I can forget it. I can live without it. But if I find it again, I'll be called back to the sea, and there'll be nothing I can do.'

She held his gaze, then reached across the table and put her hand in his. Her fingers were warm.

'Go and put it away now, hide it from me, and then in the morning, come back here and take it far away. The further it is from me, the easier it will be for me to forget it.'

She left his hand in his, their fingers caressed each other for a moment, and then settled together on the table. Warmth enveloped them along with the new silence. He was moved to go and find the skin, already in his mind where he could put it this evening, but he wasn't ready to move just yet, and she wasn't ready to let him go.

'Who was the woman in the bar?' he asked after an amount of time that had been both short and beyond measure.

'Woman?'

'There was a young woman in the bar. Seemed to come out of nowhere, left a little light behind, then disappeared again.'

She smiled, then shook her head.

'I don't know about a woman in the bar, but if she left a little light, then she knew what she was doing.'

'It wasn't you?'

'Did she look like me?'

'No.'

She smiled. 'Well, I can't explain it. There's always a little magic in the air around here, though, don't you think?'

They shared the smile – confused though he was, how could Baxter do anything but smile – and then he looked curiously at her.

'I hate to ask but… did you understand… did you understand everything I said to you all this time?'

The smile stayed on her face, eventually she nodded.

'Yes.'

'Oh my God,' he said.

'I liked it. I liked the way you talked to me.'

He thought of things he'd previously said, quickly tried to banish them. Where was the newspaper headline for this moment? *Seal Turns Into Woman In Latest Turn Up*.

'Leah is with the television man?'

'I think so.'

'You're all right?' she asked.

He lowered his eyes for a moment. Leah. That was strange.

No, not at all strange.

Since coming in here and looking out over the pool he hadn't given Leah any thought. Leah, the previous constant. Three years, when even things that were not related to Leah, would still be framed around her. How he would tell her, or what she would think.

And now, half an hour it had been, and Leah was gone.

'Yes,' he said, in answer to the question.

'Good. I was worried. You looked sad.' A beat. 'You always look sad.'

'I must have said so many embarrassing things.'

She smiled again.

'Yes,' she said. 'But I loved it. If you hadn't…'

She let the words go, but he felt them as sure as she'd spoken them.

He squeezed her fingers. Steam from the mug rose across her face. Sinatra was singing. Here was Baxter the daydreamer, and here was his dream.

April In Paris

I met the actress at a dinner with mutual friends. We sat next to each other. As usual, in a group of ten people, I wasn't saying much. She was attractive, and I wanted to talk to her, but she was mostly engaged with the two women to her left. Conversation between us did not come naturally. Still, eventually it came, and it turned out we'd both be in the west end of Glasgow at a similar sort of time the following Tuesday afternoon, and I said, casually, 'Maybe we could have coffee,' and she surprised me by saying, 'Sure, I know a place,' and she named the place and the time, and then more or less just turned away and went back to talking to her friends. That was how I came to have coffee with the actress.

*

I arrived ten minutes early. There was a sign inside the door. Order at the counter. The place was quiet, only two other tables occupied. A bright space, wooden floor and tables, all painted in worn-white, suggesting the seaside. The décor was quirky, but not nautical. There was the head of a fox above the door to the toilets, a cubist painting of an indeterminate building to the left of the counter. Billie Holliday was playing. April in Paris.

The girl behind the counter smiled, and I said, 'Can I have a coffee, please,' and she said, 'Milk and sugar?' because it was in the days before coffee came in a hundred different formats, and I said, 'Just milk, please,' and she said, 'Sit down, and I'll bring it over,' because it was also in the days when you could order a drink without your server automatically asking if you'd like a variety of food options to accompany it.

I took a seat in a booth by the window and looked out onto the street. A sunny afternoon, bright out of nowhere, the morning's cloud having vanished over lunch. I checked my watch, noted there was no sign of the actress approaching, and then looked around the café.

There were three booths by the back wall, and three by the window, another three or four tables in between. There were a couple of women sitting at one of the booths by the wall, both of whom were eating cake. They seemed to not have much to talk about.

Perhaps they'd been meeting in here once a week, every week for years, and had run out of things to say.

If I looked straight ahead, I couldn't really see the people sitting at the far booth by the window, due to the high backs of the benches, but there was a mirror on the back wall, positioned to reflect the light of the street, and in that I could see the top of a man's head, and the face of the woman sitting opposite him.

His head was lowered, as though he was looking at something. Nowadays one would assume it was a phone. Back then, I guess it was a book or a newspaper.

The woman had long blonde hair and was wearing sunglasses, her chin resting in her hand as she looked out of the window. The glasses were large and obscured more than just her eyes, but she was sitting, elegantly positioned, wearing red, as though posing for a fashion shoot.

I watched her for a moment, then looked around the café again. The sun picked out the dust particles. The two women were still not talking. Billie Holliday was still singing April in Paris. By the side of the door to the toilets was an ornamental tailor's dummy, painted as the torso of a woman, red and yellow, in the style of Mucha. The woman at the counter had her back turned, busying herself at the coffee machine.

I had the sudden sense of being in an arthouse movie. A David Lynch film perhaps, and the woman behind the sunglasses was Laura Dern, coolly looking out at the street, waiting for nothing in particular to happen.

I looked back at her, and there she sat, unmoving, posed and poised, watching the world outside the window.

I always remember the strange sense of liquidity, seconds ticking by, somewhere, on some clock or timepiece, but not in that café. I've checked since, and Billie Holliday's April in Paris only lasts three minutes, but that three minutes seemed to go on a long time. I didn't think to look at my watch.

There was movement behind me, the moment snapped out of nothing, then there was the actress, approaching my table with a purpose that suggested straight from the off she wouldn't be staying long.

As she walked to the table, and sat down opposite me, I got a flash of a prosthetic leg emerging from beneath her light raspberry gingham dress, then she laid her small bag down on the seat beside her and swept her hair back from her face.

'I'm not late?' she said.

'I was early,' I said.

I was about to explain that I'd already ordered coffee, when the waitress appeared at the table and placed the mug in front of me. A plain white mug, coffee with milk, no creamy texture on the top, no pattern of a leaf or a heart.

'Can I get the same, please?' asked the actress, in response to the waitress's raised eyebrows.

'Sure. Sugar?'

'No, thanks,' said the actress, and the waitress turned away again.

We watched her for a second, as we briefly clung to something to do before talking to each other, and then looked across the table.

There was a moment, which might have lasted a long time if ending it had been up to me, but she'd arrived with a purposeful air and wasn't about to let it go.

'I don't have long,' she said. 'I have a thing at two-thirty.'

'What kind of thing?'

I wouldn't ask that now, but I was young. The words were in my mouth, and then out into the world before I could stop them.

She looked a little non-plussed, but before I could apologise, she made a small hand gesture, and said, 'I work at a supermarket.'

It was a bad start to the conversation. A bad start to the date, such as it was, but I suppose we both already knew. This wasn't something that had anywhere to go.

'That's not really a thing,' I said.

'Everything's a thing,' she said. She was a little irritated.

'I thought you were an actress?'

She was about to respond, but stopped herself. Perhaps she could see the conversation quickly descending into irascibility and decided to be the one to stop it happening. I'm not sure why I couldn't have done that, but those edgy words just kept appearing, whether I liked it or not. Like I was interrogating her.

My wife says I still do that, even now, so I guess it's just who I am.

She held her hands apart and said, 'I'm an actress. You know how many actresses actually make money? I need to live.'

I nodded, finally ended the cross-examination, then lifted the mug and took a sip.

It was good coffee.

There was one of those temporary blips in a conversation, particularly when at least one of you is not entirely sure why you're there. I knew why I'd asked her – she was beautiful and alluring, and the kind of woman that drew men in – but I had no idea why she'd agreed to come.

There was no spark. Spark does not need to involve any romance, of course. Spark can happen anywhere, between anyone. You hit it off, you don't, any interaction can go either way. But I'd known, sitting beside her at dinner, there was no chemistry. Didn't matter how attractive I found her, didn't matter how much she drew me in, she saw nothing in me, and I, beyond her beauty, did not really see an awful lot in her.

'A strange thing happened a couple of weekends ago,' she said, the words suddenly appearing, as though she herself was surprised by them. She must have really wanted to fill that gap. I'd been about to blurt out a stupid question about her prosthetic leg, which was really none of my business, so it saved me from that.

'Yeah?'

'Yeah. Strange.'

She nodded to herself, although she was looking at me, as she thought about this strange occurrence. I took another drink of coffee.

I was waiting for her to tell me about the strange thing, but obviously my face didn't have the right setting, because she said, 'You want to hear about it?' as though I might not.

'Of course.'

'OK.'

Her coffee arrived, the waitress placing it on the table.

'Thanks,' said the actress.

The waitress smiled. I watched her turn away, then glanced in the mirror. Laura Dern was still sitting in the same position, chin in her hand, sunglasses on, staring out of the window.

There was something about Laura Dern.

'Gentlemen prefer blondes, huh?' said the actress, and I turned back quickly, embarrassed she'd caught me looking at the woman two booths over.

'Sorry,' I said, but stopped myself making some lame excuse about staring into space or looking at the fox's head. 'Something strange happened?'

'Yeah,' she said, and she took a drink of coffee, and nodded to herself again. 'I live in this large house up the other side of Great Western Road. It was mum and dad's. They died… both of them died a couple of years ago. Cancer.'

'I'm sor –'

‘It’s cool. Shit happens, right?’

The raw pain of it was evident in a few short words, but she didn’t want to talk about it, which was understandable. I was just some guy she’d agreed to have coffee with. Her parents’ death was obviously something that had just needed to be included in the story.

‘At some point dad had started converting the loft. It was looking great. He’d floored it. He’d had big windows installed on two sides, so it was bright and airy, and a million miles away from the creepy loft of your average horror movie. And there was a set of stairs leading to it from the upstairs landing, so no dodgy loft ladder or anything. Then he got ill, and you know how it goes. The loft never got finished.’

‘You haven’t tried to get it done?’

‘Don’t have the money. Really, I’m bouncing around in this huge house, and I should sell it and buy a one-bedroom. If I did that, I wouldn’t have to do seven-hour shifts working the till at the Co-Op.’

‘But it’s where you grew up and you can’t bring yourself to do it yet.’

‘Pretty much.’

Her face relaxed a little, she got lost in the thought of it for a moment, and then shook her head, and returned to the story.

‘So, I keep a couple of boxes up there out of the way, but you know, I never really go up there. Then one day, Sunday afternoon, I was upstairs, practicing a part I was going to audition for. Memorising the lines.’

‘What was the part?’

‘Doesn’t matter. Didn’t get it, don’t want to talk about it. Anyway, I hear a noise in the loft. I stop. Get a bit of a tingle, ‘cause I’m right underneath it, and then the noise continues. A bit of a kerfuffle, but not… not a big noise, not like there’s a person up there.’

I guess I was making a bit of a worried face at this point, because let’s be honest, no one wants to hear an unexpected noise in their loft, and she nodded.

‘Right? It was terrifying. I mean, we’ve all seen The Exorcist. Noises in the loft are how movies start. Thank God, and I mean, seriously, thank God it was broad daylight.’

‘Did you go up there?’

‘Sure. I mean, I had to, but I really didn’t want to. Just one of the downsides of living alone in a big-ass house.’

‘Was it mice?’

‘Too much noise for mice.’

‘Rats?’

‘I was thinking rats. I get up there, and I mean, I walked so slowly up those stairs…’

‘Did you take a weapon?’

‘Nah. I read somewhere once that the problem with brandishing a weapon is that, if you’re not trained to use it properly, you’re liable to get it taken off you, and suddenly you’re getting beaten over the head with a rolling pin. So, no weapon.’

She took another drink.

‘And what was making the noise?’

‘Two hooded crows.’

I tried to picture what a hooded crow looked like. Then I tried to picture two hooded crows in an attic.

‘Hooded crows?’

‘The grey ones, but their heads and wings are black. So they’re black and grey.’

‘Are they big?’

She puffed out her cheeks and let the air out through closed lips.

‘You’re telling me. Are they big? You should see two of them in a confined space. I mean, the loft is, like I said, bright and airy ‘n all, and spacious, but hooded crows are not meant to be inside. So, two of them together like that, in a room, they are bigger than you think. They grow to about twenty inches, I looked it up. That’s not kicking the tail off of two feet. Wingspan’s over three feet. That’s a decent-sized bird.’

‘They get in under the eaves?’

‘Ha!’

‘What?’

She took another drink of coffee. Her eyes had widened a little. Warming to her narrative.

‘That’s what everyone says. But there are no eaves. Wait, yes, there are eaves, the house has eaves, but there’s no space. There’s no gap in the walls. I don’t know if dad closed it up or anything when he was fixing up the loft, but at no point in the five years since he paused work on it, at no point have we had anything in there. No other birds, not so much as a sparrow. And I noticed in the last couple of weeks since I’ve been looking, there’s not even a dead fly or a spider’s web. It’s like a completely sealed room, nothing in or out. Mum hated spiders, and I remember dad saying to her not to worry, that he'd make sure all the nooks and crannies and holes were filled in.' She paused, then added, 'So, no, there's no way in under the eaves, not for any bird, and certainly not for something as big as a hooded crow.'

'You must've left a window open,' I said.

It was the only other option. Even if she hadn't remembered leaving the window open. Although, of course, she would have noticed when she went up.

'I've had this conversation so many times in the past two weeks,' she said. 'The same conversation every time.'

'Everyone says what I just said?'

'They do.'

'And what do you say?'

'Like I already said, I really never go up there. I never open the windows. Honestly, I haven't opened the windows up there since dad died. Not until I opened them to get the crows out.'

'No one had tried to break in, maybe…'

'The windows were all closed. There was no sign that anyone else had opened one forcibly, then closed it again.'

'So, how did the crows get in?'

She lifted the coffee cup to her lips and took a drink, her eyes on me the entire time.

'That's what's strange,' I said.

'Exactly.'

'There was really no way for those two crows to get into the loft?'

'None.'

'Who else did you speak to?'

As soon as that question was out of my mouth, I felt a bit awkward, wondering if I was going to get another taste of her contempt, that she might translate it as me asking her if she'd spoken to a man.

'I spoke to Uncle Tom, dad's brother. He'd helped him with the loft conversion.'

'What'd he say?'

'He had no idea. In fact, even though I told him I'd never opened the windows, I knew he thought I must've opened the windows. Or that I was making it up. You know, my family… everyone else, dad, mum, Tom, mum's brother, they're all professional people. A couple of lawyers, that kind of thing. And here's me, working in a supermarket, eternally waiting for the acting breakthrough.'

'You're the black sheep?'

'Yep. They all think I'm a bit flaky, and me calling Tom with this story of two large crows in the loft just fit their narrative.'

'So, we have a locked room mystery, except no one's been murdered.'

She thought about this for a moment, then nodded.

'Yes, I hadn't thought of it that way, but that's good. I like that. Yep, it's the Speckled Band, but with crows and no dead bodies.'

'And what d'you think the answer is?'

She took another drink, then laid the cup back on the table.

'I was going to ask you the same thing.'

I hadn't been expecting that.

'Why?'

'You're a writer, aren't you? I thought Alice said you were a writer.'

'Yes.'

'So, you must have an imagination, right?'

'Everyone has an imagination.'

'But yours must be better developed than other people's, though, right?'

'Why?'

'You're literally using your imagination in your job, every day.'

'I suppose.'

I didn't then have much confidence in myself as a writer, so wasn't entirely willing to buy into anything that might set me apart from anyone else. It did genuinely seem to me that anyone was capable of any flight of fancy, and that they could then write it down. The only thing that separated me from them was that I'd made the positive decision to devote myself to making a living from it.

'So, what d'you think?'

'Really?'

With a different person, or perhaps with two completely different people, this could have been an interesting conversation; engaging, maybe flippant and fun. Instead, it felt like a challenge. I'd been set a task, and my reaction to the initial question had only increased the sense of it. The tension in it.

I thought I understood it now. I'd had that feeling sitting

here, listening to the endless Billie Holliday song, something in the air, the sense of the surreal. And now it had arrived, in the hands of a one-legged actress with a strange tale of two hooded crows.

Still, there was something about Laura Dern.

'You've got a locked room, no way in or out,' I said, forcing conversation to stop myself glancing in the mirror.

'Yes.'

'And from nowhere, two large birds, hooded crows, appear in the room, at the same time.'

'Yes. Weird, right?'

'What have you thought of so far?'

'I asked you first.'

She took another drink of coffee.

'You're really going with I asked you first?'

'Yes,' she said, taking the question seriously. 'If you really have no idea, and I can't believe a writer would have that little inventiveness, then anything I say will prejudice your thoughts. You'll be less likely to come up with something original. So, what's your basic, you know, your gut reaction? What d'you think?'

She took another drink. I followed, giving myself a little more time.

I had nothing, so I answered the question honestly, even though I knew she'd be unimpressed.

'You must've left a window open,' I said.

She laughed, a sound somewhere between bitter and rueful, accompanied by the required head shake.

'Unbelievable.'

'It's just the way it is,' I said, defensively. 'There's literally nothing else. Sure, in locked room mystery stories, there are always clever criminals, some strange thing from the imagination of the writer. But this isn't fiction. This is you, in your loft. No one's being clever. Unless someone put them there as a joke.'

'There we go,' she said, 'you came up with something. Someone put them there as a joke. At least it's a suggestion. But no, that didn't happen. They were free in the loft, and they started making noise out of nowhere in the middle of the afternoon, when there hadn't been anyone else in my house in weeks. I've thought it through, and there was just no way for someone to suddenly release two crows in the loft at that time, when I'd been awake and wandering around the house all day.'

We stared at each other across the table. She took another drink of coffee. I got the feeling she wouldn't be here much longer. I guess she'd regretted agreeing to the drink, but hadn't wanted to leave me sitting here, waiting for her.

She laid the cup back down. It was empty. I was barely halfway through mine.

'What else have you got?' she asked.

The question had an air of finality about it. This was my last chance.

I stared blankly across the table.

'What else have you got?' I asked, as I had nothing.

I still remember those words, and how much I wished I'd had something else to say. Which is odd, because it's never bothered me that I didn't see her again, apart from sitting in a cinema, and being surprised she had a very small part, with no dialogue, in Harry Potter And The Deathly Hallows: Part 2. It turned out she'd also been in the previous two movies, though I hadn't noticed at the time.

Her lips positioned themselves in disappointment, her body made a small precursor move to getting up, then she said, 'Hole in space-time.'

We did that thing where we stared at each other across the table.

'A hole in space-time?'

'Yeah, look, I know, it's far-fetched, and it's ridiculous, it's whatever you want to call it. But there was no way for those two crows to be in that room, there just wasn't. It doesn't make sense. Therefore, it has to be something absurd, something incredible. You write fiction, don't you?'

I answered with sort of a nod.

'Then you must believe in the possibility of the incredible. You must.'

I've given that notion a lot of thought over the years, and I don't think it's necessarily the case. There's plenty of down-to-earth fiction. And there must be people who write the fantastical, but don't believe for a second it could happen. Yet perhaps she has a point. Why do any of us make anything up? Why is it that we create stories?

I didn't have anything to say. I lifted my cup and took a drink, nodding as I did so, perhaps to imply that yes, I did believe in the possibility of the incredible, but even I didn't know if that was what I meant.

She gave up on the conversation, and the brief chat over coffee with the guy who she was never going to see again, with a well-meaning acceptance. She smiled, then she reached across the table and squeezed my hand. Perhaps that was a move she'd learned in drama class.

'I'll get the coffees,' I said.

'Oh, right, you sure?'

'Yeah.'

'OK, thanks,' she said. There was the suggestion of a gap between the word thanks and the actual end of the sentence to imply she'd been about to say my name, and then couldn't remember it.

She smiled again, she got to her feet. There was a movement behind her, a flash of red, and I wanted to look, but the words *gentlemen prefer blondes, huh?* were still hanging over the table, and so I kept my eyes on the actress.

'See you around,' she said.

'Yeah,' I said.

And with that she was gone.

I waited until I was sure she was clear of the shop, then I looked in the mirror. Right enough, Laura Dern was no longer there. The guy was, his head still lowered, but the woman in the sunglasses had left.

I looked out onto the street to see if I could see her, but there was no sign.

Then I caught a final glimpse of the actress as she turned a corner. I wondered if she was really going to work at a supermarket, or whether it had been an easy excuse.

I turned back to the café, relaxed. The tension had evaporated with a snap of the fingers, and I stared into my half-finished coffee. It had really become too cool to enjoy, and I decided I'd order another.

The atmosphere had changed, but I don't think it was the actress who had taken it with her, despite her tale of the crows. The music had moved on, and now it was Buck Clayton's Lonesome that was playing.

That tune always sticks in my head for days when I hear it.

The waitress stopped by.

'Everything all right?' she asked, lifting the actress's empty cup.

I wasn't sure whether she meant with the coffee or with my

relationship with the actress, so I said, 'Can I have another coffee, please,' and she smiled and said, 'Sure.'

*

I've never been able to come up with an explanation for those two crows. A locked room, neither a hole in the wall, nor an open window. No way in or out, and then, out of nowhere, two large birds.

I tried writing it as a movie treatment once, to see if fictionalising it would help me come up with ideas, but it didn't work. The unfinished – indeed, barely started – movie treatment still sits in the Unfinished Work folder on my desktop.

I went back to that café a couple of times, but there was no Laura Dern.

By Douglas Lindsay

DI Buchan

Buchan
Painted In Blood
The Lonely And The Dead
A Long Day's Journey Into Death

The Barber, Barney Thomson

The Long Midnight of Barney Thomson
The Cutting Edge of Barney Thomson
A Prayer For Barney Thomson
The King Was In His Counting House
The Last Fish Supper
The Haunting of Barney Thomson
The Final Cut
Aye, Barney
Curse Of The Clown

Other Barney Thomson

The Face of Death
The End of Days
Barney Thomson: Zombie Slayer
The Curse of Barney Thomson & Other Stories

DS Hutton

The Unburied Dead
A Plague Of Crows
The Blood That Stains Your Hands
See That My Grave Is Kept Clean
In My Time Of Dying
Implements of The Model Maker
Let Me Die In My Footsteps
Blood In My Eyes
The Deer's Cry
A Winter Night
I Am Multitudes

DCI Jericho

We Are The Hanged Man
We Are Death

DI Westphall

Song of the Dead
Boy In the Well
The Art of Dying

Pereira & Bain

Cold Cuts
The Judas Flower

Stand Alone Novels

Lost in Juarez
Being For The Benefit Of Mr Kite!
A Room With No Natural Light
Ballad In Blue
These Are The Stories We Tell
Alice On The Shore

Other

Santa's Christmas Eve Blues
Cold September

Printed in Great Britain
by Amazon